PLOTS
AND
PLANS

PLOTS AND PLANS

TATA BOSBOOM

To order additional copies of this book, contact:
Xlibris
1-888-795-4274
www.Xlibris.com
Orders@Xlibris.com
739865

Dedications

For Stevie D., Dorline, and Steve DeC.

A very special thank you to Robyn and Richard Lipetz and Ruth Kafka, George Karalekas, Irma Fisher, Warren Weideman, and the Weingrads, for their friendship and support.

Also, thank you to Dave and Diane Kalinoski and all my wonderful nieces and nephews who have been so supportive.

Chapter 1

The shabby apartment was out of place in this upscale building.

There was a time when it was beautifully furnished, with art objects tastefully placed about, but all had been sold to supplement his small monthly income. There was a time when it was filled with scintillating conversation, but nobody came by anymore.

I heard something, Martine, he said teasingly to his wife. *Yes, my love, I heard something on the radio that piqued my interest. I just caught the tail end of it, so I need to catch it on the TV. If it's what I think it is, I might be able to jumpstart a great plan. My biggest and best.* He punched the air vigorously with his fist. "I'm afraid I'm going to need help on this one because I can't do it alone. Is that okay with you?"

She didn't answer. She was dead.

He often chatted with her, bouncing ideas and answering his own questions, giving himself the courage to go on.

I promised you, Martine. I promised that I would make it big one day, make you proud of me. Now I think I've found a way. They will finally realize just how clever Emmett really is.

He missed his wife dreadfully; but he remained in the apartment, keeping it exactly as she had left it, feeding his memories of her. He wanted to score while she lived, but he never did. He wanted her to be proud of him, but nothing ever worked. Every deal had soured as he lost the money they could ill afford to lose. Still, she was always there with encouragement. "Perhaps next time, darling."

Her weak voice haunted him, and like a gambler hooked, he continued his search for the "big deal."

Pushing the hassock with his foot, he slid it closer to the television and plopped down on it, then reached over, and turned the set on. The last scene of a movie played, and it was too soon to turn up the sound. He placed the pen and pad in his lap and rested his chin on his fingertips, which were held together like a man in prayer, then waited, and watched several frames of silent pictures. He had seen the familiar reruns so many times he knew the accompanying sounds: the high-speed chase with police sirens wailing, screeching to a halt in front of the drug lord's limo, uniformed men leaping out, firing orders and guns, ducking behind their wide-open doors for cover. The sharpshooter finally hits the fuel tanks, and the bad guys were blown to bits.

Slanted sheets of rain hit the dirty windows, cleaning them. The storm shook and rattled them furiously, but his eyes never left the set. If he could use this news story to activate a plan, it might give him the success he craved after a lifetime of bad breaks.

His face held very few laugh lines. Instead, it reflected the failure and despair of approaching his golden years without having made his mark in life. Time and money were running out on him.

But a rush of excitement settled in his groin as his dark eyes focused on the TV with hypnotic intensity, patiently waiting. Patience was never a problem; luck and timing were! He'd seen the doorman's eyes sliding over his shabby clothes that smelled of neglect, with food and body odors wedged in the warp and woof of his sparse wardrobe.

He glanced at the living room furniture, flimsy and worn, with soil marks like Rorschach tests imprinted into the arm- and head rests. If his plan worked, he would redecorate, hire the window washer, buy some clothes, and start tipping again. The building's staff was not as attentive since his wife's death. A successful ballerina and generous tipper, she'd given him stature and credibility in spite of his many failures. Without her loving care, he was lost; and he became seedy, a pariah in a hi-rise of wealthy achievers, barely able to scrape up the monthly rent.

Her lovely face floated before him, landing right on the TV screen. He blinked to force it away. Not now, darling. I'm not ready for you yet." He was not a religious man, but he said a silent prayer, squeezing his eyes shut. *Help me accomplish something before I die. Let me do it for Martine. Let me do it for her!*

The turkey gobble of the phone jolted him. He rose instinctively to answer, then changed his mind, annoyed at the intrusion. *Who the hell could that be?* he said aloud, knowing it could only be his aunt or a wrong number. The answering machine clicked twice, and the voice came through.

"Emmett, it's Aunt Rose. I haven't seen hide or hair of you. Are you all right?" The concern in the elderly voice would have touched the hearts of many but not his. "If you're home, pick up! Pick up, Emmett." She paused. "Well, maybe not. But call me when you get in, whatever the—" The machine cut her sentence in half.

Why does that pest have to bother me now? he muttered. *I don't have time to listen to her complaints. Besides, she makes me beg for my own money—money that's rightfully mine.* He was bitter but could ill afford to alienate her. *I was out of town, that's all!* He threw his hands up with finality, satisfied with his excuse.

He returned to the vinyl hassock and reached over to turn up the sound. The commercial was on now. Goofy little scrub brushes skated across the screen, sucking up bathroom germs like vacuum cleaners. *Whoooosh, whoooosh, whoooosh.* The bathroom sparkled, matching Emmett's glittering eyes. He dared not blink, not wanting to miss a thing.

The commercial ended, and a no-nonsense music piece heralded the eleven o'clock news. His breathing became rapid as he readied himself, Bic in hand, pad balanced on one knee. The familiar face of the pasty-faced anchor filled the screen.

"Good evening. Tonight the police subdued a machete-wielding homeless man on a train. Passengers cowered in fear as he held everyone at bay, injuring several people. It was a virtual nightmare for the passengers. We will now switch live to Carmen Ruiz at the scene."

Back and forth, the anchors read the local and international news off the teleprompters, and the sports and weather would be next.

Darn, they're not going to say anything, Emmett muttered. *I guess it wasn't that important to anyone but me.* But just as he said it, the female anchor dropped her eyes to the desk and read from the paper.

"A forty-seven-year-old woman gave birth to her first child at Oakbourne Medical Center, pioneers in in vitro fertilization. Oakbourne's fertility clinic is world renowned for their successful embryo implants. Women in their fifties and sixties have had successful treatment at Oakbourne, but there is a sad twist to this story." The anchor continued as Emmett listened, jotting things down furiously and keeping up with every word. "The baby is on life support," she concluded.

He reached over and snapped off the TV, remaining on the hassock for a long time while he reviewed his notes. He looked up and saw his reflection in the darkened screen and liked it. For a few seconds, he daydreamed of being a TV celebrity and mumbled to himself, *I'm so much smarter than all those TV hosts and weatherman. How do they do it? How do they get there?*

Then his computer mind took over, analyzing everything, thoughts never crashing but gracefully sidestepping one another, falling into place, filing in the missing pieces of the intricate puzzle that would be his grand plan. He lived for plots and plans, the excitement, the planning, and the anticipation. Then came the disappointment when things fell apart and sometimes everlasting hope when another idea would invade and capture his mind. It was his private world, where no one else was allowed.

All I need is luck. That's all I need. I was lucky to have heard that news story today. It might be a sign that my biggest and best plan is just around the corner. He rose and did a little two-step, snapping his fingers like a modern-day Henry Higgins. *I think I've got it! By george, I've got it!* He approached his

3

desk, his finger moving down the directory until he found it under *H*. He quickly punched the numbers on the telephone and waited, hoping someone would answer. Someone did.

"Hello, this is Emmett Phillippi. I apologize for the late call, but it's imperative that we meet first thing tomorrow."

Chapter 2

Janet Husking hadn't seen her baby. He was premature and placed in pediatric NICU immediately after birth. But after all these years, she had finally done it. After all the injections, drugs, scope probings, and scheduled sex, she had done it.

This birthing room was cheerful, a far cry from the stark delivery rooms of the past. Except for the antiseptic smell, it looked just like home, and everything took place here. Her son was born in a room covered with pink and blue minifloral bouquets, tied with streamers flying high like kites, giving the room a serene, protective, homey atmosphere. All equipment was stored out of sight in a large gray armoire the second it was no longer needed. A plush blue chair next to her bed was a convertible sleeper for her husband, and the empty bassinet awaited the arrival of her little son.

It had taken Janet a long time to arrive at this cheerful depot, and she was pleased with herself. She was pleased that after four long years, she had finally given Edwin a son.

At first, their life together seemed good, but Janet had become increasingly depressed. Her husband ignored it, hoping it would go away. But an obsession took hold beyond her control, and she would sob at the sight of a baby. She turned off commercials showing beautiful babies wearing Huggies or sitting in the huge donut of a Michelin tire. She refused to attend family gatherings. Her relatives were hurt and confused, and Edwin had no answers. She ceased to function.

On their twenty-fifth anniversary, she had refused to leave her bed. She lay there staring into space, muttering to herself, finding faces and shapes in the floral draperies. One face looked like a wizened old man; another face made of leaves was a pretty woman with a huge floral crown.

She stopped crying. There were no more tears left, and people change when they run out of tears. Edwin begged her to see a doctor, but they were so out of touch with each other he couldn't even bring himself to say *psychiatrist*. But she knew. "I would rather die than spill my guts out to a stranger." It startled him. She had never spoken that way before.

"Then talk to me," he pleaded.

"No." The colors in her voice sent a shiver through him as he quietly broke down in frustration. He was doing everything to help her, but she refused to confide in him. Quietly, he sobbed into his hands, the firm, muscular body wracking uncontrollably while his wife stared blankly at him, watching him fall apart. She wasn't moved; she was merely an observer.

When he had cried his heart out and his staccato breathing became normal, they sat in silence, with no word of comfort from her, the thick air churning with underlying emotion.

"I want a baby," she blurted.

His puffy eyes widened. "That's it? That's what this is all about? You want a baby?" Somewhat annoyed, he was relieved that another man wasn't involved, that a divorce wasn't imminent. He wouldn't allow anything but forced cheerfulness to creep into his voice. "Honey, you want a baby, then let's get a baby. We'll go the best agency—"

"No, you don't understand," she interrupted. "I want my *own* baby."

He hesitated, not wanting to jeopardize the headway he had made. "You're forty-seven. Even when we tried, it didn't work."

"We never tried hard enough. You couldn't wait to put your rubber back on." He was stunned at the hostility. "You were always relieved when I got my period. You never asked, but you always knew. What did you do? Count the Tampax?"

"This is all my fault?" he replied defensively.

"A baby would have taken us away from your goal," she reminded him. "You wanted to be the millionaire. Everything had to be your way. We never even had a pet!" She emphasized each word with bitterness.

"We traveled! I thought you liked that."

"*You* had the wanderlust. I didn't. I would have been just as happy staying home."

"Why didn't you speak up? You went along with everything and never complained. And now I'm being blamed for everything."

Her eyes narrowed. "I did it for harmony, but now I want my own baby! I can't be any clearer than that. I want to go to a fertility clinic, I don't care what it costs, and I want to do this before it's too late for me. Can you grasp that? Can you understand that? Am I being clear?"

He clasped her hand, eager to please. "Janet, you can have anything you want. I love you, and I'll support you in every way. You've got to believe that."

They were silent for several seconds, looking intently at each other. Then her mouth tilted upward in triumph. "You'll have to put your semen in a cup," she spoke gently.

"My cup runneth over for you." He tried at humor, not really liking the idea at this stage of their lives. Slowly the tight smile turned to laughter as they hugged and clung to each other. "Why didn't you say so? Why didn't you just speak up? You wasted a year."

"I couldn't bring myself to speak to you about it until now—until I saw you fall apart. Then I knew you would listen. You wouldn't have listened before."

From that day, Janet Husking started on her quest. The more she read, the more TV shows she watched, the more she wanted her baby. It was like a golden carrot leading her on straight to the Oakbourne Fertility Clinic.

Sitting in the waiting room at Oakbourne gave her hope and an obsessive desire to keep trying. The walls were decorated with pictures of babies born through the clinic. Doctors held seminars in which they introduced women who became pregnant on the sixth or seventh try. She gave up her job and spent over $30,000. She would not take no for an answer.

After four unsuccessful tries, the doctors decided to use the GIFT (gamete intrafallopian transfer) technique, in which the egg and sperm are mixed outside the body before being transferred to the fallopian tube where fertilization occurs. It then travels down into the uterus where the embryo implants.

Their third IVF cycle led to a successful and uneventful pregnancy, and Janet glowed with health and happiness. Never a smoker or drinker, she did everything to remain fit, and she lost the bitterness she felt toward her husband. She often took his hand and placed it so he could feel their baby. "Better late than never!" she said. She even made needlepoint pillows and pictures with that motto, which she gave to her friends and relatives. Everyone was happy.

Her doctor suggested that she have a sonogram and an amniocentesis, but she refused. "I'll take my chances, Doctor. We're both fit. We eat right, we exercise, and I've been through so much to have this baby. There's no turning back. I'll take whatever I get. This is my one and only chance at motherhood."

"I admire your generous spirit," he said, "but I strongly advise taking these tests to detect any abnormalities. At your age—"

"What would happen if you did detect something wrong?" she interrupted.

He spoke cautiously, not wanting to frighten her, "Depending on the severity—and with your permission, of course—we could abort."

She weakened at the thought. "Oh no, no, Doctor! No, not after what I've been through. I didn't come this far and this long to abort."

"That's a very extreme situation. I'm not talking about a cleft palate. I'm talking about a severe deformity. You and your husband will have the final say. Why don't you discuss this with your husband, unemotionally? Forget what you have been through. Think about what you *could* be going through if you give birth to a baby with severe defects."

"My husband knows how I feel. He wants this baby as badly as I. We'll take our chances. I know everything will be fine. Besides, it's in God's hands!"

"Yes, but we still have some control at this stage—"

"No, Doctor, it's in God's hands."

Poor God, the doctor thought. *He will indeed get the blame if something goes wrong.*

#

Something did go wrong.

As Edwin looked at the tiny figure in the plastic cube, he wondered why God chose them. They weren't bad people. Why them? Were they being punished for something?

The infant remained on life support, against the advice of the doctors. Edwin knew how much Janet wanted this baby and what she had gone through. He had to respect her wishes; otherwise, she might slip into another devastating depression.

So it was Edwin's decision that gave the child life. He was pragmatic and looked at things unemotionally. Perhaps the doctors could lessen the deformities. Edwin gazed at the small mound of flesh that resembled a split chicken—legs open, lying flat against the sheet—a baby's favorite position. One little arm curled at his side had an IV tube taped to it.

Edwin took an accounting of the deformities. *What went wrong?* he asked himself, staring in fascination at the carved slits that would have been eyes. What was beneath those indentations that were crazy-glued shut? The deformed head, which was as smooth as a grape, was larger on one side and was without ears. A current fad of young men was to wear an earring, something his son would never do.

The IV was necessary; otherwise, the liquid sustenance would pour out of his nose. His heart was encased in an odd-shaped mass atop his chest. The skin was stretched as tight as a drum, giving it an eerie transparency that pulsated and quivered with each heartbeat, like a battery-powered toy. He also had a hernia, which was the least of it. From similar cases, the doctors felt sure that he could be mentally retarded.

Edwin stared, wondering what was beneath those slits. Perhaps they would find eyes. He was lost in thought when the doctor approached.

"Mr. Husking, we know your wife wanted this baby, but she hasn't seen him. In her mind, she is visualizing a normal, healthy baby. Why don't you give us permission to remove the life support? Lord knows what else is wrong. We can say he just expired."

Edwin shook his head. "I can't do that. She'd been asking to see him and hold him. She wants to try breast-feeding, and eventually, I'll have to tell her. But now she just thinks he's premature."

When Janet insisted on visiting the NICU, he was forced to tell her the truth. Holding her hand, he gently told her of their infant. She didn't react. Occasionally, her eyelids would droop; and she would force them open again, exhausted and beaten by fate as Edwin caressed her hand, kissing it and holding it against his cheek.

"Nobody knows how much I wanted this child, Ed. Nobody knows what I've gone through to have him."

"I do, sweetheart." He was surprised at her calm.

"What can we do?"

"I've been talking to the doctors. They have maxillofacial dentists on staff that can make a cover for his palate, like a little denture without teeth. They can graft on ears and open the slits. He may be blind, but they can insert artificial eyes. We'll get the best cardiologist and surgeon, and we'll take care of him. We're his parents." He masked his lack of enthusiasm with forced energy.

"I disappointed you, didn't I?" she said. "There it is, my big try! Your firstborn is a freak. I failed you, myself, and the child. I should have left well enough alone." She sighed with resignation.

"Hey, stop beating yourself over the head. Things happen, and we've got to face them. We'll find a solution and cope with it. Right now, he's on life support until you make a decision we can live with."

"What decision?"

"The doctors suggested removing life support."

She looked away. "Then do it."

"Oh no." He pointed his finger at her. "You see him, and *you* make the decision."

"I don't want to see him."

"You've got to see him! You can't shift all the responsibility to me. He belongs to both of us. He's our child."

"It isn't our child," she cried. "It isn't even a child."

"He's not an it, Janet. He's a baby. He's a child, and he's ours!" He spoke slowly and emphatically, "You have to see him and make a decision. I want no recriminations. I don't want this thrown up to me ten years from now. I don't ever want to go through what we went through last year." His voice cracked with emotion as he remembered her year of depression, blaming him for her childlessness. He rose and bent over to kiss her. They were tired, and he didn't want to continue the discussion. "You think it over, and I'll walk a little." He hoped she would be asleep when he returned to his pullout bed. He did not want to continue this tonight.

She knew he was upset, but she would have to try to convince him tomorrow. She was too tired now.

He went directly to pediatric NICU, where the on-duty nurse was kind and supportive, speaking as though it was common to have a deformed child. He stared at the baby for a long time and asked himself, *What the hell happened? What went wrong?*

It was a question nobody could answer. He wandered slowly past the other rooms, occasionally catching a glimpse of a happy couple with their infant. He went to the lounge, where he watched the TV news with several other fathers—fathers of healthy infants—and he heard their conversation but didn't join them. He had nothing in common with them. He hoped his wife would be asleep when he returned.

Three quarters into the news program, he heard the pretty anchorwoman speak about a severely deformed child on life support, born to a forty-seven-year-old woman at Oakbourne Medical Center Fertility Clinic.

My god. Edwin rose furiously, startling the other men. *Who the hell is leaking this to the press?*

Chapter 3

Emmett looked in the mirror, humming as he worked. He carefully parted his hair and ran the color comb through it. It had been his wife's, so he thought it was a good idea and much cheaper than a dye job. All mature people were up against those snotty yuppies these days, so it didn't hurt to look younger.

After combing through several times, the red-brown color slowly tinted the top of his hair. He left the sideburns gray because they gave him a distinguished look. He combed his hair into place and stepped back, looking at his image in the mirror. A self-portrait of disappointed dreams.

Removing the towel from his droopy shoulders, he washed his hands and rubbed off the brown spatters with some toilet paper. He lowered his head, then moved it from side to side, reviewing his handiwork. It didn't look bad. He was pleased with the result. The aging man before him looked vital and optimistic. The flutter of hummingbird wings ran through him. He always felt this excitement when an idea was springing to life.

If I could turn this idea into a deal, my final grasp at the gold ring, I could die happy. I would proudly meet my darling on the other side like the successful man I should be, not some wounded dog slinking with my tail between my legs. I will do it at all costs. I will. He gritted his teeth with determination.

After the pep talk, he rose and went to the closet, looking for his one good suit. There weren't many. He pushed some clothes to one side, finding the navy tropical wool in a plastic dry cleaner's bag. His wife's closet remained as she had left it. A shrine to the woman he loved, with scented padded hangers still holding her size 6 clothes.

He carefully removed the plastic and laid the suit out on the bed, remembering the day she'd bought it for him and the thrill he had felt, like a little boy going shopping. The lapels were narrower, the trousers shorter, but the wool was like silk; it flowed with the body. He had several good cotton shirts, saving them for special occasions like this.

He pulled off the plastic wrapper and carefully removed all the tiny pins, saving them in a small blue-and-white Battersea box that held safety pins and small buttons—a potpourri of leftovers she had collected. He yanked out the plastic strip under the collar and gave the shirt a good shake. Cardboard and tissue crackled as they fell to the floor.

After unbuttoning it, he forced his arm into the sleeve tunnels, separating the fabric with a whoosh. When he tried to button his cuff, there weren't any buttons. *Darn French cuffs,* he muttered. He had sold his gold cufflinks to pay bills. But being a resourceful man, he went to his desk, placed his left wrist down, and stapled the cuff. It worked, and nobody would see it. He did the other one. Pleased with himself, he slipped into his jacket and folded and refolded the pocket hanky until it formed a graceful puff peeking out of his pocket. He felt like a boulevardier.

Wait 'til the doorman sees me now. He looked at his watch and saw that he was running late. He would have to hurry if he wanted to get to the hospital to inquire about the baby before his meeting. He was sure that some gabby nurse would fill him in on everything.

He left the building with confidence and a sidelong glance at the doorman, who finally looked pleased at seeing him so elegantly dressed. Today he looked like he belonged in that building. He walked briskly to the Oakbourne Medical Center on First Avenue and told them he was a concerned relative. When he garnered his information, he was certain his plan would work and looked forward to his meeting with Waverly Hampton.

#

Emmett entered the diner and looked around. He saw that his guest hadn't arrived. The breakfast stragglers were starting to leave, so the place was fairly empty. "Two please, and may we have a booth?" He slipped her a dollar. The waitress didn't object. At busy lunchtime, four people would have had to share that booth while he and his guest would have been seated at a cramped table for two next to some retiree, who would eavesdrop on their conversation. So 11:00 a.m. was a perfect time.

The waiters in black pants and short yellow jackets were eating their early lunch before the hordes descended, so the waitress was the only one on the floor.

Occasionally, they would direct some remark to her in Greek. Emmett understood a few words and got the gist of it. One fellow wanted to introduce her to his friend who liked women with large breasts. She ignored them and told the counterman to tell them to shut up. She brought two glasses of water and plastic-covered menus, setting them down and ignoring Emmett while she answered in Greek. "If you're buffoons, then that's why you get lousy tips."

"I got a tip for you," one called back, and they went into gales of laughter. The counterman joined them as he cleared the dirty dishes and wiped the counter off with a damp rag.

The girl's nostrils flared, but she didn't crack a smile. Emmett hoped they would stop all this before his guest arrived. He had serious business on his mind, and this casualness would be distracting. Several customers turned and looked at them, so they settled down.

Emmett glanced at his watch. It was eleven fifteen, early enough before the stampede. They could talk without having to deal with glaring eyes trying to get rid of them, ready to seat the next shift of patrons. He glanced at the dessert carousel, spinning round and round. It was filled with chocolate cakes, cantilevered ridges circling them in thick fudge icing. He was tempted to run his finger through it and lick it off. The tall glasses held rice pudding sprinkled with brown cinnamon. An occasional dark speck was visible. *Perhaps a raisin or a fly,* he thought. The lemon meringue pies were top-heavy, leaning a little to the left. The white meringue toasted across the peaks. Half cantaloupes and honeydews racked on small plates accompanied by lemon wedges, quietly sat on white paper doilies. By one o'clock, the carousel would be empty. It spun round and round, having a hypnotic effect as Emmett stared and thought about his plan. He didn't see his guest arrive.

"Emmett, how are you?" The blond god strode to the booth and extended his hand. He spoke and moved in a confident manner, and Emmett's heart quickened at the sight of him. But it wasn't sexual excitement; it was the power he felt—the power he could attain only through this perfect man, a man made of selected parts.

He slid out and pumped the man's hand, placing his arm around him. "Way. Good to see you. You're lookin' good. Should be in the movies or the news."

Waverly Hampton laughed, not taking the compliment seriously, while the dark-eyed waitress looked approvingly at him. Emmett's eyes darted back and forth, taking in the glances of the few people there. "You're looking prosperous," the young man said.

Emmett shot a silent message to his wife: 'Thank you for this beautiful suit. He's impressed.'

Waverly Hampton: tall, blond, and handsome, with the bluest of eyes that nobody could resist stood before him. Emmett knew he had a winner, and he basked in his aura. *We should be at the Regency, having a power breakfast,* he thought. But money was tight, so the deli would have to do—for now. He knew he would have to make a quick visit to Aunt Rose and play the dutiful nephew. He needed money to pull this off.

He waved the adoring waitress away with a brusque. "Give us a minute," then turned all his attention to Waverly. "Sit down, Way. I thought we'd meet here because it's fast, and I could run my plan by you, see what you think." He looked at his gold watch, a Concord his wife had given him, the one gift he hadn't sold. He hoped Waverly noticed it. "I have another appointment," he fibbed, "so I'll get to the point." He leaned forward, his fingers steepled. He looked from under hooded eyelids and lowered his voice to a conspiratorial tone. "I have what it takes to launch your career."

The young man said nothing, waiting for more.

"We've got to act fast, though—fast!" Emmett snapped his fingers for effect. "Lightning fast! You know I'm a lawyer. I also went to Wharton, and I know a lot about business."

Waverly looked at this homely little man and wondered what life would be like behind that face. Surely, it would not be as privileged as his, but he admired Emmett's drive.

"Emmett, does this have anything to do with my candidacy, which never really got off the ground?" He chuckled amiably.

Excitement sparkled in Emmett's unblinking eyes. "It has everything to do with your candidacy. But this time, it'll take off, I assure you." He spoke with confidence, "I know you don't have big money behind you, and you're not a household name. But give me the chance, and I'll solve your problems. I'll be your mentor, your strategist, your babysitter, your campaign manager—you name it, I'll be it! I'll even run the city for you. With my legal and financial expertise and your stance, we just might be what this third-world town needs."

He avoided the word *appearance*, even though he knew Waverly's appearance would play a huge role in the successful bid for mayor. He knew that physical appearance impacts social and professional interactions, and it was something he was not lucky enough to have.

"Realistically, you may not win this time around, but you'll gain a following. People will get to know you. In four years, the next time around, the sky's the limit! This is a dress rehearsal for the next one." In his heart, he hoped it wouldn't be.

"Sounds okay to me." Waverly was amused at Emmett's intensity. The waitress hung back and licked her pencil but finally screwed up her courage to interrupt. She was polite to Emmett and flirtatious with Waverly, sending all the right female signals to him by tossing her hair back and pushing her breasts firmly against her uniform so he could see the outline of her nipples. She wanted his attention. Emmett liked that! He knew this man was a winner.

They chatted while eating chicken salad sandwiches and iced coffees.

"Where are you speaking now, Waverly? The Ys? The Pentecostal and evangelical churches? The basements of Catholic churches or senior groups nodding off before your eyes?" He chewed and swallowed and wiped dressing from his chin. He took a drink to clear his mouth and leaned forward to continue in a measured voice, "We can capture the media, but we have to move quickly. Every second counts."

Waverly watched him in silence, curious now, waiting for more.

"Is there anything in your background that could derail you as the 'Protect Life' candidate? And you must be straight with me. You have got to be squeaky clean. There mustn't be anything in your past that could pop up and haunt you."

Way pondered for a moment and shook his head. "No, nothing that I know of. We pay our taxes. I've never been arrested or involved in any S&L or insider trading scandal. You met my wife. She's devoted to me and the cause. We have no kids to embarrass us. It just didn't happen. That's why we're so passionate about prolife. I'm with an investment company, and Lily acts as my campaign manager. She's had a lot of fun doing it. Compared to others, we lead a pretty dull life."

"Good." Emmett was pleased.

"What's this all about, Emmett?"

"I found a springboard to catapult you into the homes of millions of people. Whether or not they will agree with you is another story, but they will know you. And you are a very likable chap. I'm depending on that to sway them to our side."

Emmett explained everything in quick detail about the deformed baby on life support. He added that he had been to the hospital earlier, posing as a relative, and had gotten friendly with one of the nurses, who said the baby was placed on life support against the advice of the doctors. The father was confused and didn't want to take full responsibility. But the nurse had seen cases like this where healthy people were expecting perfect children. She was certain that when the mother saw him, her disappointment would overwhelm her and she would reject him.

"And," Emmett was pleased to announce, "when I told her I was a widower, she gave me her number for updates on the situation. I suppose I'll have to take her to lunch one day. The minute they decide to remove life support is when we step in, and they *will* want to remove it. So be ready! You will assume public guardianship on his behalf because the child has the right to live. You will file a restraining order against the hospital, doctors, and parents, preventing them from removing life support. You're the Protect Life candidate, and you will protect this baby's life!"

"Hmmm." Waverly savored the idea, thinking of all the media coverage. He knew the value of that, of his name and his face all over the TV and newspapers. Talk shows, interviews, debates, possibly a TV movie even if he was defeated. His campaign was languishing with both a constant lack of funds and an amateur campaign manager who did it out of boredom and watched his every move. He needed something, and that something just might be Emmett Phillippi!

"Emmett, you're brilliant! Positively brilliant! Tell me what to do, how to do it, and when to do it, and you're on! You're my new campaign manager."

A flutter ran through Emmett. *He called me brilliant, Martine. Someone finally recognized it.* He wished they were having this meeting at some elegant restaurant instead of this dump.

"I have prepared everything." He handed Way an envelope. "Read it, savor it, sign it. We've got to have a contract. If I'm going to ride your coattail, I don't ever want to be shaken off. Especially if I make you a huge success."

"We'll shake on that," the young man said, extending his hand, sealing their bizarre pact. The waitress witnessed a historical moment in New York's political life as the luncheon crowd started to walk in, taking up the booths and tables. Chairs were scraping the floor, and jackets were hanging on hooks. Suddenly the place was packed, with a line starting to form at the door.

This was perfectly timed, Emmett thought, slipping the waitress her tip. *I hope everything else goes as well.*

He floated down Second Avenue, his feet never touching the ground. He hadn't felt this good for a long time; his life had changed with one phone call. *This is it, my love,* he mumbled, looking up. *This is it.*

He'd better start giving the old lady some attention, prime her a little for the much-needed cash to launch this scheme.

He found the key and let himself into the old brownstone. There was a musty smell. The furniture was in wonderful condition, but it was old. Everything was old and expensive, just like its mistress. He climbed the stairs to the first floor and called out like a little boy, "Auntie Rose, Auntie Rose." He walked into the kitchen and peeked into the back garden. He looked in the cluttered living room, which greeted him with the same musty smell. He went up to the small bedrooms, but she wasn't home.

Maybe the old bag died, he was hopeful. *Maybe my timing's finally right.* He chuckled as he went to the main-floor den and guestroom, then down to the basement, and laundry room, calling her name. But she was nowhere.

He went back up to the old-fashioned living room. Ecru doilies had been pinned on the arms and backs of the maroon velvet sofa, which sat between two blue velvet club chairs. Fringes lined the bottom edges like a flapper's chemise. A coffee table, covered with paperweights and snuff bottles, was placed in front. Heavy velvet draperies hung from the windows. It was a somber, dark room, not often used. What distinguished it from any other old lady's living room were the valuable paintings and antiques carelessly strewn about. Some were in vitrines or cabinets, and others were left around on table tops. He wondered how the cleaning lady could cope. *She probably doesn't even dust in here,* he thought. They'd never even realize the value of anything. It was a mishmash of beautiful things one could not fully appreciate because nothing was properly displayed. There was just too much of everything. A life of collecting.

What a waste. He shook his head. *I could get so much mileage out of this stuff—all the money I need.* His eye fell on a small bronze, a winged horse about four inches high. It looked like a falconet, but the hallmark said otherwise. *If it's here, it's worth something, and I need it.*

He stuffed it into his pocket. *Darling, forgive me, but this will fetch a much-needed sum at Christie's, and it will never be missed. I need the money, and they will never ask for provenance since they know me so well.* He reached to the rear of the table and replaced the bronze with a small metal urn, the patina a lovely shade of green. He stepped away, sizing up his cover-up with satisfaction. *Now, where's Aunt Rose?*

She was always there or visiting next door. *That's it. She's next door.* He dashed down the stairs, the heavy door slamming shut behind him. He pressed the neighbor's bell impatiently waiting, then leaned on it until he saw a shadow approaching the frosted glass. He heard the peephole open and close, and then the door swung open.

"Hello, Emmett! Long time no see!"

Spinster was imprinted all over, from her porcelain skin and thin passionless lips, to the faded blue eyes rimmed with faded lashes. A blue sweater hung loosely over her shoulders held together by a chain. Glasses attached to a faux pearl necklace dangled across her small bosom. Pearl earrings clung to her withered ears, which reminded him of dried apricots, and silver waves framed a pinched face. It resembled a Martha Washington wig. *I wonder if that's a wig.*

"How are you, Millicent?" he inquired politely. "I'm looking for my aunt. Is she here?"

"Ohhh..." She sighed dramatically. "You mean you haven't heard?" Before he could respond to that, she added, "By the way, I'm not Millicent anymore. I'm Melisande, you know, like the opera."

"No, I didn't know." He backed away, not wanting to be trapped. "But what haven't I heard?"

"Would you like to come in and visit?"

Knowing he would be trapped, he quickly declined. "No, thank you, Millicent. I'm in a rush."

"Melisande," she corrected.

He rolled his eyes. "Melisande. Look, I need to speak to my aunt."

"She's probably down the block with new best friends.

"Some friends," she said sarcastically. "We had sort of a falling out, so she picked up with that homeless bunch at the end of the block." She poked her head out of the doorway and pointed. "Down there, near Second Avenue. They come from the shelter and congregate there begging, using filthy language, urinating, and littering all over. Someone said they even had sex in that little park. Can you imagine? She gave *me* up for them. A bunch of homeless bums!" She was indignant. "You haven't been around much, Emmett. You really should come around more often. You don't know what goes on." She held up her fingers, counting. "Rose gives them money, clothes, and shelter and even lets them use her shower. Then she treats them to lunch at the diner. She doesn't have time for me anymore. She just has time for that homeless bunch, trying to reform them. A lost cause, if you ask me."

Emmett was quietly taking it in. "You're kidding, right?"

"No."

"That old fool," he mumbled.

"She's not an old fool. She's havin' the time of her life, and she doesn't care if she ends up with lice!"

"Oh god, they're that bad?" he said with disgust.

"Worse!"

"Then she'll get herself killed."

"I don't know about that, but she will get lice, that's for sure."

"Well, I'll put a stop to that." He turned on his heels and shot off like a rocket toward Second Avenue.

That was rude, Millicent said to herself, offended at his abrupt departure. She stepped out onto the sidewalk and watched him stride briskly toward the diner in the afternoon sunlight, which wasn't too kind to his hair color. *Gee,* she thought watching as he approached the corner, *I wonder if he dyes his hair. It looks like it was colorized by Ted Turner.*

#

Emmett saw his aunt leaving the diner, chatting amiably with three men and a woman who were thanking her for the wonderful meal. They were a scruffy bunch. Even from this distance, he could see the unhealthy pallor of their creased faces—the dull purplish brown caused by life on the streets, drinking, and drugs. *Where did she dig up these misfits?*

He shook his head at their shabby, ill-fitting clothes. One man wore grimy checkered polyester pants, with the black dye smearing into the white checks. They were high waters, hitting his ankle several inches above his shoe. The woman wasn't bad looking, but she was painfully thin, and her jeans sagged. Her short brown hair had some gray running through the uneven cut. They all wore windbreakers and sneakers, probably from a Goodwill bin.

Nobody noticed Emmett as he drew closer, his eyes fixed on his aunt. She was a ringer for Mrs. Clause: a short roly-poly woman with a mop of gray curls and metal-framed glasses on a pert little nose. The glasses kept slipping down to the round tip of her nose.

One of the men had a toothpick sticking out of his mouth. "Beats the soup kitchen," he said with a belch. The scruffy bunch surrounded her as she quickly handed out bills like a mother goose giving her brood their allowance.

A purple wash spread over Emmett's homely face as he saw his inheritance going to some homeless shelter. *The woman is mad! I'll have her committed! How could she give these lowlifes money when I need it?*

Up the block, Millicent was still watching, getting an eyeful, glad that her former friend had been caught in the act with these social misfits. *This is better than the soaps,* she muttered.

"Aunt Ro."

She looked up in surprise, then cast a beady eye on her nephew. "I phoned you last night, Emmett. Where were you? I could drop dead, and you wouldn't know a thing." She was on the offensive.

"I'm sorry. I was out of town." She looked at him unbelievingly. "I was," he protested. Then he gestured to the group surrounding her. "What do you think you're doing?"

"Having lunch with friends," she said, a defiant tilt to her head. "You don't visit, so I made new friends, and they're not as dull as that stupid Millicent." She introduced him, "This is my nephew Emmett, my sister's boy."

The four nodded and mumbled, then shuffled about, feeling the tension, hoping he wouldn't spoil their good deal with the old lady. He ignored them and firmly took Aunt Rose's arm, steering her back to her house like a truant child. She shouted good-byes over her shoulder. "Come by tomorrow, you hear!"

She's giving these leeches money, and I have to beg. I'm glad I took the sculpture. I'll blame them, he plotted, feeling the small bump in his pocket.

Millicent, who had been spying, quickly retreated indoors, leaving her door ajar so that she could hear Rose get what-for.

"You let these people in your house?"

"Yes, she replied, unabashed, "they're very nice. They've all suffered misfortunes, and I'm helping them. They're my friends and a lot more exciting to be around than some people I know. I have great plans for them. I have a very good business mind, which has never been put to use, and I have wonderful ideas. And we'll implement these ideas very soon."

"Why don't you lunch with—"

"Millicent," she interrupted, "who now calls herself Melisande." Then, in a mock haughty tone, she said, "She goes to bridge and the Republican Club only to meet a man. I've had a man. I don't need that. I need friends, and I get great pleasure from helping them!"

"Help *me!*" he said, preying on familial ties as he helped her up the steps. "I'm your flesh and blood."

"I've helped you time and again!" she answered sassily. "Have you forgotten just how many times I've helped you with your crazy scheme? How many deals and schemes have you been involved in that never worked? I lost every cent. And what about your education, which, may I remind you, your uncle and I paid for? And you couldn't even make a living. You're an educated derelict, Emmett. Thank god your wife had brains and talent, and thank god she had insurance. Otherwise, you'd be in here with me. And I don't need that. I need my independence." She unlocked the door, and they entered the brownstone.

"I need money, Aunt Ro," he whined. "It's only fair."

She turned to look him squarely in the eye. "The minute you get your hands on money, it's gone. *Poof*!" She gestured with her hand.

He said nothing but felt resentment. *Half of that inheritance is mine,* he thought. *It should have gone to my mother. Half belongs to me.* But in his most sincere insincere voice, he muttered, "Just be careful, Auntie Ro. I do worry about you!"

"Huh!" She laughed. "Don't think I believe that for a minute."

"What a terrible thing to say." He put on a wounded look. "I do worry about you." He had to convince her, but it was her money he really worried about. He needed that more than anything to pull off this deal, and he didn't want a bunch of strangers getting in the way, taking anything that was rightfully his. "Aunt Ro, if you continue to be frivolous with your inheritance, I'll have you declared incompetent. The neighbors will back me up."

She turned to him, steely-eyed. "Don't threaten me, Nephew. If you ever mention anything like that again, I'll disinherit you."

Emmett quickly apologized, and at that moment, he fully understood the true meaning of the golden rule: "He who has the gold rules."

Chapter 4

Ever since she was little, Janet Husking dreamed of a perfect pink baby just like the dolls she played with. Her nieces and nephews were perfect, so she never dreamed she would ever be confronted with such a horrible problem.

"This is not my child," she said firmly when she saw the baby for the first time. "There is no way I could ever bring something like that into the world. He's not my child. Somebody switched my healthy baby for this freak. It's happened before."

"There was no switch, Mrs. Husking," said the doctor. "If you like, we will give you the results of DNA testing." They wouldn't let her languish in denial. She had to face reality.

She was embarrassed to have presented Edwin with such a firstborn. She felt unfit and wrestled with terrible mood swings that made her turn on the bewildered husband. "Why did you allow life support? Why didn't you finish it? Did you want to rub my nose in it? Edwin's right again?"

He handled the unpleasantness with equanimity. "Honey, I had no choice at the time. I knew how desperately you wanted a baby, and I couldn't do it. You would never forgive me."

"Well, I can't forgive you *now*!" She was striking out at everyone for nature's great mistake. "I don't want it." Her body convulsed with sobs. "I don't want it! Pull the plug. Pull the goddamned plug!"

There was a desperation in her voice Edwin had never heard before, the polite veneer of the past washed away in the tears and sweat of this ordeal. She left the hospital the following day, still insisting on removing life support.

#

When Emmett called the nurse he had befriended, she promptly fed him the details, hoping for a date. He was eligible. Then the very eligible Emmett fed the information to the media.

"News flash: A tragic turn of events for a couple who for years desperately sought to have a baby. Last week Janet Husking gave birth to a deformed premature baby boy at Oakbourne Medical Center. Now the distraught couple is seeking to remove life support."

Programs and articles examining the moral issue suddenly flooded the public. "This is worse than abortion. This is murder!" some cried. "Older women who want companionship in their old age should stop having babies. This is a typical case of an aging woman who can't handle the problem. They are not righteous people. Here is a woman who wanted a child, paid dearly for it, and now, because it isn't perfect, doesn't want it."

That was the cue for Waverly Hampton, the protect-life candidate. "You don't arbitrarily destroy a life because you're disappointed in his appearance," the handsome man asserted. "If that were the case, most of us wouldn't be alive today. This is an ego trip for an aging woman who had everything and wanted to see a perfect image of herself. Now, because the baby is not perfect, throw it out!" He charmed the TV camera with his Caribbean blue eyes. "Therefore, I have stepped in as public guardian serving the parents, doctors, and Oakbourne Medical Center with restraining orders preventing them from removing life support. This baby has the right to live, and I am protecting his rights."

Waverly Hampton was so gorgeous and so sincere that public opinion was on his side, even though two-thirds of the people disagreed with him. Emmett was the conduit establishing relationships with members of the press, making inroads, answering questions, and, most importantly, returning calls. He opened the lines of communication with the media, and Waverly charmed them. When interviewed on television, they were asked, "Why are you interfering with the Huskings' personal life?"

"Interference," Waverly said thoughtfully. "That's a good word. I am running interference for that child. If I don't, he'll be dead."

"Why should you play God?" another called out.

"I'm not. I went through the legal system. And God wouldn't have to do that." They laughed.

Another reporter asked, "Do you think it's morally right to prolong the life of an unfortunate infant who will never be normal?"

"We don't really know that. Having a handicap or a deformity is no guarantee that a person can't have a good mind. There are many brilliant people working in research and academia who wouldn't fit into our description as physically normal, but they still function very well." He pointed to another reporter.

"It seems to me, sir, that you're a busybody interfering in someone's private life."

Emmett glared at this woman who was young and attractive. Waverly focused his blue eyes on her and said, "You have every right to say that. I am interfering but only because this woman went out of her way to bear a child at great risk and great expense. She refused medical advice and all testing beforehand, so certain was she that her child was prefect."

"How do you know that?" A question shot out at him.

"Mr. Phillippi, my manager, uncovered that fact. Now," he continued, "because that child is imperfect, should she be allowed to discard him? Shouldn't the Huskings make some attempt to correct some of the defects, spend some of their fortune to give the little guy a fighting chance? If it doesn't work, so be it, but give him a chance. That's all I ask."

"Mr. Hampton, have you seen the baby?" This question came from someone Emmett had planted in the audience.

Waverly came through with the practiced line: "Yes, and he's a feisty little guy."

The press picked it up, giving them a title: THE DO-GOODER AND THE FEISTY LITTLE GUY. Goodness emanated in every photo of him, and Janet Husking looked like a shrew. It didn't help that she refused to answer questions and glared at the press. They called her "this humorless, sullen woman."

"That's a little harsh, folks," Waverly said, coming to the rescue. "Mrs. Husking has been dealt a severe blow, and I will try to help them handle it."

#

"Who is this person?" Janet shrieked. "Who is this interloper? A stranger who doesn't know us or anything about us? And he's going to help me handle it? How presumptuous. He's a total stranger. How can a stranger invade our privacy? Where is our right to privacy?"

"You lost it," said their lawyer. "He has assumed public guardianship of your child, protecting his right to live. He has petitioned the court and has served the papers."

"But we're the ones getting stuck. It's not fair."

Edwin shot a look at her, shocked at her choice of words. Gone was the gentle woman of the past. These events seemed to unleash a hidden facet of her personality.

The lawyer was firm. "Mrs. Husking, the responsibility rests on your shoulders. You refused all prenatal testing against the advice of your doctors, saying you'd take what you got!" He rubbed her nose in it.

It was a harsh thing to say, but it was a fact, and her face contorted as she tried to explain what she felt. "I never dreamed that two such healthy people would end up with a freak. That's what it is, and I don't think we should suffer the rest of our lives because nature screwed up. We were sincere about having a baby, but this is not a baby."

"I'm afraid he is. Parents have gotten stuck since time immemorial because of nature's screw-ups. Your 'little guy,'" he said, quoting the press, "is here to stay. And as long as Waverly Hampton is in his corner, you can't do a thing about it. All eyes are on you, so beware of what you say and what you do."

She glared at him but said nothing more.

"You're paying me for advice and counsel, so I will give you my advice. Put a lid on all your comments. 'No comment' is sufficient for now and smile sadly once in a while. Don't antagonize the media. Refer any questions to my office. Have I been clear?"

"Perfectly," Janet snapped. "I have to keep my mouth shut while that windbag makes us look like murderers."

"That's right, Janet," the lawyer answered. "This is a very sensitive issue. If the press hadn't got wind of it, and Waverly Hampton hadn't stepped into the picture, the doctors would have removed life support. They told me there was no hope for a normal life. He's premature, and without life support, he would expire in minutes. If you have acted sooner instead of bickering about who should make the decision, you wouldn't be in this situation. Legally, Hampton is the public guardian of your child, and legally, you no longer have the authority to make a decision ending life support. As you so succinctly put it, you're stuck. Now, my advice to you is to be sad rather than angry or rude to the press."

But the advice came too late. The Huskings were portrayed as monsters and Waverly Hampton as the white knight! He gave television and magazine interviews. His flamethrower of a voice melted the hearts of women. Even those who felt he was an interloper were charmed by his good looks and noble effort. "He shouldn't be involved, but he does seem sincere, and I think he really believes he's doing the right thing."

The Huskings began to get threatening mail and horrible phone calls. "You wanted a kid, bitch! Since it ain't a carbon copy of you, you want to toss it, like garbage. You have a responsibility to that kid. He ain't garbage. You are!"

"You should die instead of the baby. Someone should kill you."

Edwin longed for the old days before the maternal fixation. He was afraid to answer the phone after someone threatened them.

On and on, the media circus raged. Way Hampton was becoming a household word, appearing on every program, with his likable, easy manner. Emmett was elated at the results of his own strategic planning to make Hampton a success. His own success rested on that.

Chapter 5

The sculpture Emmett had pilfered from Aunt Rose brought him a few thousand at Christie's. He was an old client, after selling off all his own valuables, and they knew him, so there were no questions.

But he needed more money, so he decided to drop in on his aunt. After using his key to gain entrance, he heard voices in the kitchen and knew immediately that that a bunch of rapscallions were there. He decided not to be too harsh; if discovered, he could always hang the thefts on them.

"Aunt Ro," he called and heard the shuffling of feet and the scraping of chairs on the ceramic tile floor.

"We'd better go, Aunt Rose," he heard one of them say.

My god, now it's Aunt Rose? Next she'll be adopting them. Still, he had to be cool. After all, things were going well.

She answered him guiltily. "Emmett, what a surprise. You might call next time. My friends were just leaving."

He caught the scent of coffee, the street, and urine as they rose to leave, saying their good-byes. They shuffled down the stairs and slammed the outside door behind them.

"I'm warning you, you're going to get lice or fleas or whatever they have," he told her.

"I will not. I let them shower and use the washing machine, the poor things." She caught herself before she said any more.

"Does Winsome know about these characters?" he asked, refereeing to her sassy cleaning woman.

"She doesn't mind," she lied, knowing full well that the hardworking cleaning woman despised them.

"Tell that lazy white bitch to get a job like I have," Winsome had said. "Don't let those sweet-talking street punks take advantage of you 'cause they only talk sweet to you when they want something. Otherwise, their language is filthy." Winnie was not an ally.

"You're playing with fire, Aunt Rose. These people are crack addicts and thieves. They're not like the Bowery bums of your era: colorful, harmless drunks. These people are dangerous. You're going to end up dead one day!"

"So be it! We all end up dead one day!"

He thought of bringing up the missing sculpture to blame them, then decided not to rock that particular boat just yet. Somehow, though, he had to get rid of them. "Did you see my man on TV?"

"Yes, he's very handsome. But why is he doing that?"

"He believes the child has the right to live."

"Oh, pshaw. That poor baby has the right to die in peace. Why are you interfering? I cared for your uncle many years, so I know what it's like. The child will never be normal. It should be allowed to die, and you should keep your nose out of other people's business. I know you, Emmett! You couldn't care less about the baby. There's nothing altruistic about you. You only visit when you want something." He clenched his fist in anger as she hit a nerve. "And it must kill you to see me helping those people because you want it all for yourself."

She had been sassy ever since she'd been letting those losers hang around. He was planning to ask for money but thought better of it. *I'll fix her, Martine. I'll just take something.* He changed his approach. "Do you still have pictures of me as a youngster? *People Magazine* is doing a piece on the man behind Way Hampton. That's me! We're going to get him on the mayoral ballot."

"*People Magazine?*" Suddenly, all the unpleasantness was forgotten. "Do you need one of me too? I'm your only living relative! There's a picture of you on a pony when you were seven, and I'm standing beside you. How you cried, afraid of that pony. That's why I had to stand there. You were a sad little boy."

"Of course I was sad. My mother was estranged from the family. Do you think I didn't feel that? All the kids spoke of their grandparents, and I had to pretend mine were dead."

"Perhaps, if you were a pretty little girl, things might have been different," she said wistfully. "You might have wormed your way into his heart."

"But I wasn't!" he angrily snapped at her, remembering his unhappy childhood. "I was a homely little boy caught in the middle of a family feud. A child surrounded by selfish, despicable adults."

"Oh, Emmett, your parents loved you."

"No, Aunt Ro, they lusted for each other, whenever and wherever, and I was just in the way."

"Now, that makes sense," she spoke thoughtfully, staring vacantly at the wall. "I always wondered what that marriage was all about. He had to have something to capture that blonde angel."

"Not to me, she wasn't," he replied bitterly. "Martine was my angel." Then, suddenly changing his voice, he continued, "Now, be a good girl and get those photographs."

"I know exactly where they are. I used to look at them all the time, but I'm too busy now." With that, she clambered up the stairs and went directly to a guestroom where she had stored family memorabilia.

He quietly walked into the hallway and lifted a small Dufy painting. *How's this, love?* he asked Martine, quickly stashing it into his briefcase. Like lightning, he removed a small painting from the infrequently used living room. He would bring a cheap dime-store copy next time to replace it. As long as there were familiar paintings on the wall, nobody would notice. It was not the most convenient way to get money. He'd have to go to Christie's, then wait for a check, but it was the best he could do for now.

A short time later, Aunt Rose slowly descended the stairs, lugging a shoe box crammed with loose photos. He ran over to help her.

"Put those in the kitchen," she commanded. "We'll go over them together, perhaps have a bite to eat."

He didn't want to get stuck and knew it would take hours to go through all of them. "I have a meeting with some PR people. You go ahead and choose a dozen good shots of us, and I'll be by in a day or two. I trust your judgment." He bent over and kissed her curly head, then picked up his briefcase, and left, yelling over his shoulder, "I'll lock up. No need for you to come down."

A few moments later, she was engrossed in the project, choosing suitable prints and placing them in three piles. Good—bad—maybe. "Oh dear," she muttered, *"People Magazine!"*

Chapter 6

The deep debilitating postpartum depression that Janet Husking suffered made their lives intolerable. She felt an overwhelming sense of despair that was compounded by the fact that she did not want the baby and would not agree to continue life support. The baby lived only because of Waverly Hampton.

When this became known, courtesy of Emmett, there was public outrage, and they were inundated with more calls and threats. They were forced to change their number, and Edwin refused to open any mail. The company he worked for wasn't happy with the bad press and suggested a leave of absence. He hired a security guard for their protection. With so many crazies around, one never knew. He was drowning in guilt and sorrow for not having been an enthusiastic partner years ago. He felt that he was being punished.

Janet lay in bed, barely eating, staring into space with vacant eyes, not uttering a sound. Ghastly thoughts invaded her mind. Suicide, murder. *How easy it would be to drown him, to hold his head under water for a few seconds.*

Edwin finally convinced the doctor that it was more than "baby blues."

"If she doesn't snap out of it, I'll prescribe Prozac as a final measure," the doctor said. "I also suggest the support group within the hospital, women with postpartum depression. They help one another."

After being silent for days, Janet suddenly grinned.

Thank god, Edwin thought, *maybe she's corning back.*

It was a stupid grin that turned into a sly smile, and the corners of her mouth tilted upward until he heard the hiccuping of laughter. It pleased and frightened him, and he didn't know what to make of it. Tears flooded her eyes, but she couldn't stop laughing. It had the sound of a lunatic, someone who'd gone round the bend, and it continued as tears rolled down her face.

Laughter and tears. It frightened him! Edwin asked the guard to come to her room, and they watched the maniacal scene together. Edwin reached for the phone, still watching her, but she waved her arms back and forth to stop him.

"Don't, don't, don't. I'm all right. Really, I am." She could hardly speak through the laughter.

He went over to her. "Breathe slowly. Here, drink this." He reached for the glass of water on her nightstand and held it to her lips. "Slowly, honey, drink slowly. Are you all right?"

"Yes," she murmured, and after a moment, she composed herself.

"What was that all about?" He looked as puzzled as the guard.

She took a deep breath. "I thought of something very funny. You've got to listen to this. I figured the whole thing out. I wasn't lying there feeling sorry for myself. I was thinking and plotting things out! And do you know what I'm gonna do?" The men didn't respond. "You know what I'm gonna do?" she asked again with no response. "You don't know, do you? You can't even imagine it. You're too civilized, that's why." The men watched in silence. "I'm gonna give him the kid." They didn't react. "The guardian, Waverly Hampton. I'm gonna give him the kid. He wants it so badly. Let him have it. We'll see how he likes that." She fell back on the pillow, howling with laughter. "I'm not gonna get stuck. *He* will! Isn't that a great idea? I think it's great!"

A chill ran through Edwin as he envisioned the headlines: "Bitch mother gives baby away!" *When will this end, dear god, when will this end? Help me. Please help me,* he silently prayed. He didn't know what to do anymore.

Janet and her new personality took over, demanding that their lawyer carry out her wishes. "Waverly Hampton wants it, so he can have it."

"Janet, I'm telling you, there will be severe repercussions from your decision," said the lawyer. "Why don't you just allow the baby to be on life support for a while until things calm down and you're out of the news? I'm sure the baby won't live very long."

"But what if it does?" she screamed. "Do I have to pretend I like all this? Do I have to live a lie to please reporters and a bunch of strangers? I lived a lie for twenty-five years, and I won't do it anymore." All the years of bottled-up frustration broke loose, and she picked up a delicate porcelain music box and threw it against the wall. It smashed with such force that it bounced back like a ball, a gift from her past life, a gift she had received from Edwin for being a "good girl." "I can't do that anymore" she screamed in anguish.

"Do it her way," Edwin flatly ordered their attorney.

The attorney sighed in defeat. "Okay, I'll draw up the papers and call a news conference."

"Do that," the exhausted husband replied.

#

The press conference was a huge success. Everyone ate it up. They couldn't get enough. The distinguished attorney stepped in front of the microphones, then

29

looked down, and read, "Mr. And Mrs. Husking have examined all possibilities in their tragic case, and because of Mrs. Husking's fragile mental state they have decided."

Emmett was watching at home and held his breath with excitement. *We won,* he thought. *They're throwing in the towel, and Way is a national hero. We got the publicity, and they still have the kid.*

The lawyer continued, "They have decided upon the following course of action. Since Mr. and Mrs. Hampton are childless and since they have shown such interest in the welfare of our child, it is morally fitting to allow the benevolent couple to legally adopt the unnamed male infant. They have already assumed public guardianship, so the legalities of this case will be worked out quickly to everyone's mutual satisfaction."

Emmett was stunned. His face slackened, and his jowls hung like a St. Bernard's. *Holy cow* was all he could say.

The Hamptons also watched the television news and went ballistic. "That jerk! You said he could do anything. Well, he certainly did. He got us a baby—one I don't want."

"Lily, calm down." He put his arms around her. "Just calm down. This is a ploy. Emmett will think of something. There isn't a better Machiavellian mind on the planet. Just remain calm. We are becoming a household name, getting millions of dollars of publicity. You want to be first lady someday, don't you?"

She cast her sullen eyes on him. "Not if I have to take that baby."

At that moment, the phone rang. It was Emmett.

#

The baby battle drew national attention, and the first salvo was fired directly at Emmett and Waverly. It was a direct hit, and it threw them off balance. There was a steely toughness to Janet as she plotted with her lawyer. Her husband, uninvolved, hovered in the background, longing for their peaceful life just a scant four years ago. He missed his gentle wife, the woman he had lived with for so many years. He didn't know this woman.

The furious Hamptons blamed Emmett.

"You got me into this, so you get me out, dammit," Waverly told him. "Get me out. Lily's having a fit. This was not in the deal! Do something!"

"Calm down. I'll think of something. I always do. But all eyes are on you right now, watching your actions. I'll schedule a news conference, and you and Lily must be gentle and kind when you read your reply. Trust me!"

When Way Hampton stood in front of the cameras with the tangle of microphones like the Medusa's head directly in front of him, his blue eyes looked bluer and more sincere than ever. You couldn't believe that he really didn't want this child.

30

"Lily and I are so happy to welcome that baby into our lives. We chose to save him, and we welcome him with open arms and open hearts."

Bullshit, Janet thought as Lily stood beside him.

"We want to thank the Huskings for making the right decision. They don't want the responsibility, but we do. The adoption proceeding will begin immediately."

What an actor, Emmett thought. Sincerity oozed out of every pore, and he looked so damn good Emmett knew he had a winner. *We're not going to wait. We're going to try for the primaries.*

It had turned into a moral issue, and every paper and TV program condemned the Huskings for what they had done. Since the baby was still on life support and would continue to be, Emmett did everything to surround the Huskings with bad press. He made calls to Edwin's company, disguising this voice, complaining about employing "such a person." He carefully wrote a poison pen letter to the couple and leaked it anonymously to the press. When it was revealed, copycats followed. He was relentless in pressuring them into taking the child back.

He had other things on his mind as well. A vitality took hold, and his mood was upbeat and optimistic. He knew his man could do it. Waverly captured the media and could carry the vote. All they needed were the 7,500 signatures to get him on the mayoral primaries a few short weeks away.

They would have to move fast and work hard, but so far, luck was on Emmett's side; and finally, this time his timing was right. He wanted those signatures now, and he would sell his soul to the devil to get them.

Chapter 7

Winsome muttered to herself as she washed down the kitchen cabinets and picked up the beer cans that were strewn all over. "This place is turnin' into a pigsty with that bunch."

"They're not that bad, Winny."

"Salt-and-pepper trash—that's what I call 'em."

"I've seen Henry looking you over. He's not bad."

"Who's Henry?"

"The African American chap." Aunt Rose was up on things and wanted to be politically correct.

"Ms. Rosie, you oughta be ashamed of yourself. You think I can't do better than some homeless bum?"

Aunt Rose recoiled at Winsome's language. It was clear she hated the homeless and was glad there was only one of her kind represented. To her, the rest were lazy white trash, and she hated having to serve them and be polite to them.

"I don't want them touchin' or usin' the wash machine," she ordered. "I don't want lice in my machine."

"They'll be drowned," came the smart-alecky reply.

"Well, I don't like it." She wiped the cabinets harder, taking it out on them. "Their clothes stink, an' why can't that white bitch get a job like me instead of sitting in her own pee?" She turned to Rose. "I worry about you. I know all about street people, and you gonna get a rude awakenin' someday. And if you ever try to fix me up with that good-for-nothin' Henry, I'll go right next door and work for Ms. Millicent."

"You wouldn't last calling her that," Aunt Rose said. "Besides, she's a jealous old woman. Jealous that I have friends, jealous because I was married, and jealous because I got my house from a husband and not from a daddy. She was a big daddy's girl, but I know her secret."

Winsome's interest perked up. She walked over to the old woman, holding up her arms, water and bubbles sliding down her arms from the wet sponge. Did she have a man in her life? Was that her secret? She loved the soaps, and this was going in that direction.

"That among other things. But that's all I'm going to say. I have another secret." Aunt Rose loved to tease.

Winsome knew exactly how to play the old woman. She acted disinterested, and therefore, Aunt Rose was dying to tell her. It was a ploy she had used many times on the old woman.

"I have a secret too, but I ain't sayin' nothin' 'til I'm sure." Winsome had begun to notice that things were missing, but she didn't know if Emmett or the homeless people were stealing them. As far as she was concerned, they were all the same. And she worried about the old lady.

"Take a rest, Winny. Sit down and let's have tea." Aunt Rose lifted the sparkling stainless steel teakettle and took it to the sink, where she filled it up right to the top. Winsome continued her work, deliberately taking her time, knowing Ms. Rose was bursting to tell her whatever was on the mind.

"Come on, Winny, sit down," she coaxed, setting the cups and saucers on the table, dropping a tea bag in each cup. The cleaning woman worked slowly, and Ms. Rose couldn't contain herself. "Winny, I have a plan."

"Am I in it?" the sassy cleaning woman teased.

"Maybe. I've always had a good head for business."

"What?" came the startled reply.

"I never worked," she quickly added, "but a lot of my ideas came to pass through other means. Now I'd like to try my hand at a real business, for my people. I'm going to open a department store for them."

"What?" The incredulous woman had to grip the table and sit down. She was thunderstruck. Her arms slipped off the table and dangled at her sides, water and suds running down and forming little puddles on either side of her. "If you goin' to do that, why don't you put *me* in business?"

"We can do that too. Start a charlady service."

"You mean I gotta clean house while you open a department store for some crackheads? That ain't fair!"

"It certainly is." Aunt Rose tossed back her words. "Winny, when you hear this, you'll prefer cleaning, I guarantee."

Winsome peered at the older woman, lowering her eyes and challenging her to explain. "You plannin' to buy Macy's?"

"Oh no." Aunt Rose laughed. Gray curls bounced like springs as she shook her head.

Suddenly they felt the draft of the downstairs door opening. "Aunt Ro," Emmett called.

"Up here, Mr. Emmett."

Winsome rose immediately to head him off at the landing.

"I think your aunt's gone coo-coo," she whispered, circling the air with her forefinger next to her right ear. "She's gonna buy a department store for those good-for-nothin's that hang around her."

Emmett's eyes widened. "What say? Did I hear right?"

"You sure did. A department store!"

"God, there goes my money," he muttered. With renewed vigor, he walked briskly into the kitchen to confront his aunt. "I'll stop this right in its tracks."

But she wasn't there. Somehow, Aunt Rose managed to disappear right from under their noses. They looked at each other and shrugged, wondering where she had vanished to.

"She knows she's in trouble," Emmett said sternly. "If this foolishness continues, I'll be forced to take over her finances." The thought made his eyes glitter. It was evident that he liked the idea.

Winsome watched with a wary eye, sorry she had ever told him about Ms. Rose's crazy idea. Now she had two things to worry about: Emmett trying to gain financial control and the homeless whose raunchy speech and behavior miraculously changed when the generous old lady was around them. *Yes,* Winsome thought, *I'll keep a watchful eye. They'll have to go through me to get her.*

They heard the shuffle of her scuffies on the stairs and remained silent as Aunt Rose cheerfully appeared carrying an armload of clothes.

"All right, young lady," Emmett said, "is it true you're going to open a department store for that homeless scum?"

"Don't patronize me, Nephew. You're still wet behind the ears. And yes, I am, and why are you so interested?"

"Why indeed! For starters, I need money. We have a baby to care for, so why not help me?"

"Oh, Emmett," she said with a laugh. "Is that what you're worried about? Money? My department store won't cost me a cent."

Emmett and Winsome looked at each other and rolled their eyes.

"Our department store will be on the street," Aunt Rose continued. "You know the scaffolding in front of those old buildings on Thirty-Fourth Street? It'll be perfect. We'll put a table there with all the garments on it. It'll be a store for the homeless, run by the homeless."

"That's it," squawked a disappointed Winsome, "a street store?"

"Yes, that's it." She waited for their comments, but they said nothing. They were not impressed. "It'll be a street store for the homeless. Right now, most aren't welcome in stores. Some of them do smell, and some might have bugs... but not my people. It'll be a subeconomy within their community, run exclusively for them. That'll make them feel special. I'll get a vendor's permit, and we'll collect used clothes and items—anything. We'll fix things, mend, wash and iron clothes, then sell them at a very low price. It'll be their own business, and perhaps they can expand to other area. You see, Winsome, I have the ideas, but they'll have to run it. I'm teaching them responsibility. They must have regular hours, regular pickups, merchandise repairs, and washings available."

"Not in my machine!" Winsome protested.

"They will keep books, take inventory, learn about business."

"You hope, Auntie," said Emmett. "But my guess is they won't last a day. What do you think, Winny?"

"I think I won't be shopping there." The teakettle burbled, sputtering water instead of whistling. It was too full, so Winsome turned it off and poured some of the scalding water into the sink. "I told you not to fill up the kettle. There's no room to whistle. It just spills all over." But the old lady paid no attention. She was engrossed in the plans for the new store.

"Emmett, you still have all those old clothes from your lovely wife?"

"Put that out of your head, Aunt Rose. I won't part with any of Martine's clothes. To see some smelly tart wearing her exquisite silks is beyond imagination. You'll get nothing from me."

"Emmett," she said sternly, "Martine is dead. Stop living in the past. Come out of your mausoleum and join the living. Your wife's clothes could do a lot of good. She always helped people, including you, and her generous spirit could continue, if you would only cooperate."

"No! The answer is no!" he replied tersely.

"All right. I'll remember that. But you remember that I can be just as tough as you." She turned on her heels and disappeared through the basement door. The cool, musty air greeted her as she carefully carried her inventory down the steps to be sorted and laundered for the new store.

Winsome poured hot water into the cups. Perhaps a cup of tea would calm things down. Emmett didn't seem unhappy with her presence as he had been in the past. He would never lower himself enough to drink tea with the cleaning woman.

Now he needed an ally, and he presented a strong case to her about taking over his aunt's finances. Winsome listened patiently, nodding her head and saying "uh-huh, uh-huh" at the appropriate times.

But inside, she was forming her own silent objections to him. The more he elaborated and the more excited he became at the prospect of handling millions of dollars, the more Winsome was determined to do everything in her power to talk sense into Ms. Rose to rid herself of her homeless friends and to prevent a takeover by this ambitious man.

Chapter 8

"Mr. Phillippi cancelled again," their lawyer informed Edwin Husking. "It's the second time now. This time he's sick."

"He's stalling," Edwin said angrily, clutching the telephone as if it were at fault. "Playing for time."

"We know that, but the public doesn't, and you're still getting bad press."

Edwin spoke thoughtfully and honestly, "I'm also taking the heat from my firm. They had a meeting about this. The firm's name has come up in the press, and they've had calls from old money clients to do the morally correct thing. There are a lot of right-wingers with great wealth. The meeting we had was a veiled threat to my job. They don't like adverse publicity."

"Would you consider stopping the adoption?"

"I would, but Janet is adamant. I don't know what to do," he spoke almost to himself.

"For now, do nothing. I'll be in touch." The lawyer hung up, feeling more sympathy for Edwin than he did for the other players in this drama.

Emmett hoped the bad press the Huskings got would pressure them to change their minds. He was equally under tremendous pressure from the Hamptons, especially Lily, who was becoming jealous of her husband's success without her guidance.

"Your brilliant Emmett isn't so smart, after all," she nagged. "I would never have compromised you like that. He'd better get us out of this one, or he'll end up a permanent babysitter."

But Waverly approved of everything Emmett did. The results spoke for themselves, and they were astounding. Contributions poured in from around the country. Foundations and organizations for handicapped children were especially generous. They wanted a voice in politics, and they made that clear with their support.

There was enough money for Emmett to rent a storefront on Third Avenue for campaign headquarters and assemble a group of volunteers. He would try to stall the adoption as long as possible and proceed quickly with the signatures while they continued getting good press. Waverly was a Johnny-come-lately, but he could do it with Emmett's help. They needed more volunteers to man the phones, so he asked Aunt Rose and Millicent if they would help. Millicent retaliated against Aunt Rose's snub by refusing, saying Emmett was using that unfortunate child as a tool to advance himself. She felt the child should be left to God, and Emmett was gaining the reputation of being a P. T. Barnum. He took advantage of anything and anybody to gain media coverage to promote his candidate.

He made frequent trips to his aunt's house to pilfer. *If she is so generous to that crummy bunch, she could be generous to me,* he rationalized to Martine.

#

Romayne "Kiwi" Quieter did the laundry for the group when Winsome wasn't around. She had showered, and small damp ringlets formed all over her head, her bangs a curly fringe across her forehead. Her high cheekbones and delicate features gave her an exotic look. She wasn't a bad looker for a forty-two-year-old homeless woman. Her skin was murky from all the alcohol and drugs, and she might even have AIDS. Who knew? She had been servicing the guys in the group and would do just about anything to be taken care of. After tasting the good life at Aunt Rose's, she was hoping and planning to get off the street one day.

She started to visit Aunt Rose more often without the men. After a leisurely shower, she would lounge in the guestroom, pretending it was her house, longing to live in it. The old lady was nice enough, but she'd had her chance. Now, Kiwi felt it was her turn.

She also thought about Emmett. He was homely and older, but so were some of the other men she had sex with. And Emmett would inherit everything one day. Maybe he would get to like her if she had sex with him. She could teach him things—lots of things—please him. She had survived the streets that way, servicing men at an early age. If she did it with Emmett, maybe he would take care of her. All the women did it that way. It was easier than working in Rose's street store, standing around for hours behind tables of old clothes. Being confined to one spot all day held no appeal. She was cunning and pragmatic as she planned her future.

She was still daydreaming when the noisy old washer spun to a halt. Aunt Rose insisted they wash their clothes and smell clean when she took them to the corner diner to discuss their plans. Kiwi bent over, lifting the heavy wet bundle. Aunt Rose had never replaced her old dryer, so she had to hang them on the clothesline it the basement. The tangled mess of sleeves and pant legs looked like a swirling mass of copulating octopi.

Slowly, she tried untangling them. The whites were still a grimy gray. The darks had tiny white specks of a forgotten tissue all over. *Shit.* She was losing patience and was becoming frustrated trying to untangle the mess and pick off the white specks. At least they smelled better.

Suddenly, she heard voices upstairs and was glad the washer had stopped. She could eavesdrop.

She heard Emmett's voice. *He looked at me more than he should,* she fantasized, and now that she was clean with curly hair—well, perhaps if he saw her—he might want sex. Perhaps he would fall in love with her and take her off the streets. He could be the answer. She could live here in this grand old house.

She heard Aunt Rose talking about some big deal he was involved in, something about the mayoral election. Kiwi thought if she could help him win, maybe he'd marry her. Then she wouldn't have to put out for alcohol and drugs. *Think of something, Kiwi,* she urged herself as she left the tangled bundle and tiptoed up the stairs and put her ear to the door.

Emmett was giving his aunt an update on the baby, the adoption, and the 7,500 signatures he needed in less than a week. He was getting volunteers to help. Then he asked for a loan. "This is it, Aunt Ro. Don't let me down!"

"Have I ever?"

"No, but this time, I need ten thou."

She sighed and shook her head in exasperation. "I do wish you'd get a paying job. There's a lot to be said for a steady weekly check."

"What about your homeless bunch?"

"Emmett, this is philanthropic. I am trying to introduce them to a nicer life, encouraging them to seek employment to get that life. Never mind my people, Emmett. What about yours? What are you going to do about that poor baby?"

"We'll adopt it, of course. That's why I need the money."

She chuckled. "You must have pooped a brick when they threw you that curve! I'm sure you're hoping someone will get you off the hook."

Suddenly the door swung open, and Kiwi burst in.

"My god," Emmett exclaimed, staring at her, "you're spying on us!"

"No, Emmett," a calm aunt Rose explained. "She's not a spy. When Kiwi has a thought, she just barges in before she loses it." Her pen was poised, ready to write the check, so he didn't pursue it. "What is it, Kiwi?" the old lady gently asked.

"I... I... I had an idea," she stammered. Her thoughts were quicker than her words.

"See, I told you." The gray head nodded in triumph.

"I... I... know how to get the names on you... you... your petition."

"You were spying," he spat out.

"The... the... the... street people can sign. The... the... they did it before. They do it all the time for money."

"You don't even have a legitimate address, you twit." He was condescending, but he watched his aunt in his peripheral vision She still held the pen and had not

38

written the check, so he changed his attitude and oozed charm. "Kiwi, is that your name? Are you from New Zealand?"

"N... n... no. My last name is Quieter." The effects of her drugs were wearing off, and she was starting to feel anxious and jittery. She began to fidget. "We can use this address. Take names out of the phonebook. They don't check—"

"Unless the other candidates file a complaint," he interrupted. But he was thinking about it. "Can you get your people to cooperate fast?"

"Give them $5, and they'll do it, and they'll keep their mouths shut."

He turned to his aunt, who was glad that Emmett was taking Kiwi's suggestions seriously. The good woman truly wanted to rehabilitate and help these people. "Can you up the ante another ten thou?"

"You only need 7,500 signatures," she pointed out. "And with Mr. Hampton's popularity, most of them will be legitimate." She knew he took advantage of every situation, but she was happy with Kiwi's involvement and her efforts to become a constructive citizen, albeit a crooked one. She wrote out the check and handed it to Emmett, who was pleased.

"Kiwi, get all your people at campaign headquarters immediately. We only have a few days, and they'll get their money, I promise."

"I haven't transferred the money yet, dear, but I trust you will keep your word to Kiwi," Aunt Rose sweetly warned.

"Of course, luv." He grabbed the check. "Thanks again, Aunt Rose," and kissing her on top of her tousled head, he lifted his briefcase and left.

Kiwi felt confident. He liked her idea, so he must like her. She was like an advisor. So far so good. She watched as he passed the living room and saw him reach in, pick up a jade elephant, and drop it in his briefcase.

She said nothing to the old lady. She would protect Emmett. He would be her ticket to wealth and security.

Chapter 9

Millicent was bitter! She felt left out, losing her old friend to that homeless bunch and all of them having the time of their lives. They were on street corners gathering signatures for the petition in and out of campaign headquarters, drinking coffee and eating plump deli sandwiches, and having a snort or a drink when no one watched. They would congregate next door in Rose's garden and talked and laughed into the night, never once asking her over.

She now regretted having turned them down. She would have had fun spending time with Rose again. But Rose was bored with her. *Rose loves being the center of attention, and just because I don't encourage harebrained schemes, she's bored with me. Huh!* she muttered indignantly. *She complains about Emmett? She's just as bad.*

She hated the lot of them as she peeked out of her kitchen window and fantasized about killing them with an imaginary ray gun. *Zap! Zap! Zap!* A smile crossed her face as she watched them. *If they only knew,* she thought. *If they knew her secret, they wouldn't want to be there. They'd want to be miles away from that thing in her garden.*

A circle of grass surrounded a cement stepping stone with a decorative raised relief pattern of a child and bunnies. Bricks were placed around the stone, and patches of grass pushed through the spaces between the bricks. It looked innocent enough, but it concealed a fifty-five-gallon drum that had been carefully buried there since 1943 when gasoline was rationed. Dr. Foster had his connections, and he never needed ration stamps for anything. *That drum was proof that Daddy could do anything.*

She was now seventy-seven years old, and still nobody knew. If they had, the neighborhood would have been in an uproar. Quiet, staid Murray Hill with its civic committee. They would have made her remove it, afraid of blowing up the block in a blaze of glory. What a Fourth of July fireworks it would make!

It was her link to the past, when her daddy could do anything. A physician to the rich and powerful, he became a power by association, and in her dreams, she heard his warning. After all this time, there was nothing left but her secret and the deadly residue in the drum. Too bad she couldn't blow them all up—except Rose. She liked Rose, and she missed her. They went shopping together, drank afternoon tea, had political discussions, and went to an occasional movie at Kips Bay. She was lonely and wanted her friend back. They were all involved with that baby; but perhaps, in time, after they used her up, she could come back.

The adoption hung over everyone's head like a dark cloud. The Huskings continued to get bad press; and they were condemned from the pulpits, on the streets, and in the news. There was a real possibility that Edwin would lose his job, and they continued getting threatening calls and letters.

Finally, he'd had enough. He decided to take matters into his own hands and told Janet, "Shut up or go it alone! You're having the time of your life. I think you rather enjoy all this—the control, the attention. If you say one more thing to the press, I'm outta here."

She backed off, knowing he meant it, and his cool head prevailed. He and their lawyers worked on a press release, retracting all statements and halting all adoption proceedings. Edwin would take full responsibility for his son.

"I'm going to hire a nurse. When this commotion dies down, I'll place the infant in a nursing facility for full-time care for as long as he lives. It'll be expensive, but at least it will stop the circus, and I'll still have a job. Now, let's get this done as soon as possible."

Janet said nothing. She knew she would have to tread lightly, but the wheels kept turning.

Edwin was adamant. Tomorrow he would arrange a meeting with the Hamptons, knowing that they would be delighted to be childless again. The disruption to his life was intolerable, and he looked forward to the following day when he would put an end to this circus.

He called his lawyer and then phoned the hospital administrator to tell her of his decision and to make certain the press would not invade the place once his announcement was made.

"Thank you, Mr. Husking," she said. "I'll take adequate security measures. I think you're doing the right thing, and I commend you for it. When all this dies down, please come to see me, and we will discuss a facility for your baby."

When he hung up, he felt good. He felt in control again. He looked forward to tomorrow, to the press conference at Oakbourne, when he would answer all their questions and get back to his quiet life.

#

There was always orderly confusion at shift change at the hospital. The coming and going of staff added to the unsettled atmosphere for a short while. Then everything ran silky smooth again.

At 3:10 p.m., the day shift was preparing to leave, rinsing out their mugs, clearing their desks, going to the restroom to freshen up. The night shift was preparing for duty. Staff and private duty nurses, aides, cleaning people, volunteers, and visitors walked the corridors.

Nobody noticed the elderly nurse hovering outside pediatric NICU. She wore a light-blue sweater with an ID tag pinned to her uniform. A blue mask dangled like a small bib in front as she peered through her glasses at some papers. She was indistinguishable.

When she walked inside the unit, the on-duty nurses looked up but went back to their monitors and charts. *Just another curious body,* they thought. The flashes of lights and the hum of life support systems kept them company but dulled their senses at the end of the tiring day. The two women sat behind a large round elevated desk overseeing the unit with tired eyes. Five of the eight isolettes were occupied, with the Husking baby in the middle. The elderly nurse left.

At 3:25 p.m., one of the nurses went to the ladies' room and was promptly whacked on the head as she entered. She crumbled into a white laundry pile, a bump the size of a wooden darning egg forming immediately. The elderly nurse ran to the desk.

"Your friend passed out in the ladies' room!"

"I can't leave this unattended."

"She's hurt and callin' for you. I'll monitor. Now hurry."

The nurse rose and backed away reluctantly, then hurried to her friend. The second she left, the elderly nurse yanked the plug on the middle isolette. The tiny body twitched spastically. To the relief of the intruder, no beeper sounded, and there was no battery-powered backup. The problem showed on the monitor, but no one was there to see it.

The elderly nurse left immediately. She got on the elevator to the first floor and hurried to the ladies' room where a bag was stashed behind the trash bin. She went into a stall, threw a light raincoat over her clothes, left the building, and lost herself on the crowded street. Pleased that she had taken charge.

There would be no more controversy—the baby was dead!

Chapter 10

"My god, Ann, what happened?" The shocked woman ran over to her friend, who was lying on the cold tiled floor. She knelt beside her, grasping her wrist and taking her pulse. She ran the cold water full force and grabbed a handful of paper towels, soaking them and putting the dripping paper on her co-worker's forehead and wrists.

An on-duty nurse entered. "What happened?"

"I guess she fainted."

The cold water and equally cold floor helped revive her. Finally, her eyelids fluttered, and she opened her eyes and saw the two figures beside her, looking down in her face.

"What happened, Ann?" her friend asked gently. Then she tossed an order to the second nurse, "Get some more cold towels but wring them out. We're making a mess."

The woman responded, careful not to slip on the puddles around the prone figure. Water still dripped from the makeshift dressings.

"Someone whacked me, I swear it!" said Ann.

"Who?" the shocked woman asked.

"I don't know. But I think it was that nurse."

"The one that came into NICU?" They helped her sit up.

"I caught a glimpse of blue, and she wore a blue sweater."

"But why would she hit you?"

"I don't know." She reached for her bag, which was nearby, and they looked into it. Nothing was missing. "Oh, my aching head." Her hand touched the bump that had formed on the side of her head.

"We'll need to get some ice for that. Can you take care of her?"

"I'm on duty, but I'll stay."

"Thanks, I left my babies. Maybe that maniac kidnapped one."

The more she thought about it, the more panic-stricken she became. She rushed into the unattended NICU, and a cold sweat washed through her as she hurried to each isolette, checking the babies and the units. When she reached the grasp, "Oh god, no!" she cried out to a passing doctor.

"Do something."

"What's wrong?" he replied.

"The Husking baby! Look at his color. I think he's dead."

"There was no alarm?" Others hurried over to the isolette.

"The unit is off." the doctor said, checking the lifeless mound.

"That new nurse—I know it was her." she cried.

"Who?" the doctor asked.

"I saw her," another nurse said. "She wore a blue sweater."

"Right. She covered for me when I went to the ladies' room."

"I know who you mean. I saw her." another doctor added.

"And she's gone?"

"Yes, she'd gone."

"She lied to me," the nurse cried. She feared the consequences of leaving her post more than of the child's death. "She lied to me and killed him."

"Call security and seal the building," one of the doctors yelled. "Don't let anyone leave."

#

The blue sweater that had hung around the shoulder of a murderer ten minutes ago was now hanging on a hook in the main-floor ladies' room. Mrs. Kramke, who had come to visit her niece, was almost trampled by a vision in black making a hasty exit. When Mrs. Kramke entered the stall and closed the door, she spotted the light-blue sweater and quickly stuffed it into her tote bag even before she urinated.

Finders keepers, she told herself. *Maybe that tank left it. It'll serve her right.* She stopped at the mirror to comb her hair and patch up her makeup before going to the fifth floor.

When she got off the elevator, she was stopped by a security guard. "Sorry, ma'am, we've had some trouble on the floor. We're canceling all visitors' hours."

"But I came from Long Island to see my niece. I can't make this trip every day."

As Mrs. Kramke's voice got louder, other visitors were lining up behind her. Suddenly the elevator door opened, and the hall was swarming with a sea of blue uniforms. The police spoke briefly to the security guard, who nodded in Mrs. Kramke's direction. The word started to buzz around. "A baby was murdered, the one that was all over the news involving that politician. She was the first visitor on the floor. Mrs. Kramke would have entered the hospital about twenty minutes ago, the same time the murderer left the building."

"But we don't know if she did leave," the doctor said.

"I'll take bets she didn't stick around."

"Ma'am," they said to Mrs. Kramke, "can I see some ID?"

"Sure, but what's this about? Is my niece okay?" As she opened her bag and fumbled for her wallet, her purse was lying on top of the blue sweater, which was tucked on the bottom of her tote bag.

"Your niece is fine, but someone just murdered the Husking baby. You must have heard about that case on the news?"

"Yeah, I did, but who would do that?"

"We don't know yet. It just happened about the time you got here. Did you see anything or anyone in a nurse's uniform wearing a light-blue sweater over it?"

Her heart began to beat faster. *Oh, dear god, if they find the sweater, they'll blame me.*

"No. I went to the ladies' room downstairs. And a woman in a hat, pants, and black raincoat—you know, like a lightweight trench coat—banged into me, rushing to get out. But there was no one in a uniform."

"Will you come with me, Mrs."—he looked at her ID—"Kramke?"

They took her down the hall to the lounge where the police had taken over, displacing all visitors. The two NICU nurses were sitting there. They looked up at the detective and Mrs. Kramke with no sign of recognition.

"This lady came in about the time the murderer left," said the detective. "She saw a woman in a black coat leave the first-floor ladies' room. Could our murderer have done a fast change? It makes sense. Everybody would be looking for a uniformed nurse wearing a blue sweater, and people can very easily move from floor to floor."

He ordered his men to search the ladies' room, and Mrs. Kramke went along to make sure it was the right one. They found a large plastic bag in the garbage, not the usual stuff you'd find in a hospital bin. But it was empty.

"If this belonged to the person," said the detective, "she could have stashed the bag there, picked it up when her dirty deed was done, and just pulled on slacks and a coat over the uniform... wearing gloves, I might add. But check the bag anyway."

Mrs. Kramke wondered if she should tell them about the sweater she'd found, but she was so frightened she started to shake thinking about it. So she said nothing. Besides, she liked the sweater. After several more questions, she was given a pass and allowed to see her niece. She prayed that she would get out of there without complication.

The long arduous task of interviewing hospital personnel and visitors led nowhere. Nobody could give a clear description of the nondescript murderer. An aide remembered the blue sweater but nothing else. They questioned the on-duty nurse repeatedly, hoping she would remember something.

"I'm sorry, Detective, I just can't tell you any more. I'm trying so hard to remember, but it all happened so fast, and now I'm in hot water for leaving the floor. The woman said she was a nurse, and maybe she was. Maybe she was a nutty nurse! She wore a light-blue sweater over her uniform, and she had an ID tag pinned on. But I never read it. Would you? There was an emergency, and I responded as quickly as possible. As far as I know, I left my post to another nurse."

The Huskings never had the opportunity to read their retraction. When reached with the news, they reacted stoically yet relieved that their problem was no longer a problem.

"It's over, Ed," Janet said when they were alone.

"Yes, it is... in more ways than you think."

She arched an eyebrow at him. "Let's not double-talk anymore."

"I don't know you, Janet," he said bluntly. "The woman that I just got to know, I don't like."

"So you're saying you want to leave?"

"I don't know. I'll tell you if I decide to do that. I have no doubt in my mind that you can handle it."

"You're absolutely right. I can handle it," she answered in a flat, unexpressive voice. She revealed too much of herself; it was a part he'd never seen, a part he didn't like. The marriage was unraveling.

The detective saw the Huskings as suspects, but their security guard gave them ironclad alibis. "She never left the house, and Ed was in the den with the lawyers, working on the retraction."

"They could have hired someone," the detective kept fishing. But after a check of phone records and bank accounts, nothing unusual was found. Since it was not a brutal murder, the police felt it might be some nut or perhaps someone with a handicapped person in their life who took matters into their own hands to put this child out of his misery.

The police found out that Waverly Hampton was taping an interview at NBC several blocks away, so detectives went to question him. They also questioned Emmett.

The newsmen at NBC couldn't wait to tell Way Hampton. They wanted to get a first-hand reaction, a scoop. They had to wait until the taping was over, and try as he could to shield his man, Emmett was rendered silent when the vultures took over. "Mr. Hampton, your baby was murdered an hour ago at the hospital. How do you feel about that?"

"What!" the shocked man replied. "Is this some joke?" He looked at Emmett for reassurance.

"It's true." Emmett pushed forward, waving his hand for silence. "Gentlemen, please let me speak with Mr. Hampton privately. I'm sure this is quite a shock to him."

They fired their next question, "The Huskings were planning a retraction of the adoption. Were you aware of that?"

"No," Emmett calmly said. "Please give me a private moment with my man. Then you can have an exclusive interview afterward." The press was hungry, and he was at a television studio, so why not take advantage?

He and Waverly were escorted to a boardroom while the reporters waited, tongues hanging out, saliva dripping like starving animals waiting for them to emerge.

"Did you know about the retraction?" Waverly asked him.

"No."

"Did you know about the murder before it happened?"

Emmett was stunned. "Is that what you think of me? You think I'm that stupid? You think I would hire someone? With all the crazies around, it could be anybody."

"I'm sorry, Emmett. I didn't mean that. I apologize. I don't care who did it as long as I'm not a suspect."

"You're a prolife candidate. Nobody would even think of you."

"I hope not," the relieved man replied.

"Guaranteed," Emmett reassured him. "You'll be fine. Try to shed a tear as we go and meet the press. Then speak calmly to the police."

NBC got their scoop. The tragedy provided a great photo opportunity, albeit a phony one.

"Squeeze out those tears," Emmett whispered. "It'll be the photo of the week." In his estimation, it was a political home run.

The police were satisfied that Waverly Hampton was not involved. On Long Island, the Huskings tried to keep the funeral private. They'd had enough of the media. Emmett begged, then insisted, that Waverly be allowed to attend. He was almost this baby's legal father; they owed that much to him.

Rather than get into another nasty skirmish, Edwin capitulated and allowed it, but he made it clear that the press was not welcome, to the disappointment of the Hampton camp.

"It's better than nothing," Emmett said as he coached his candidate, knowing he was inwardly relieved but never showed it. For the record, Waverly took the death of the baby much harder than the Huskings, who were dry-eyed throughout. When the tiny white coffin was about to be lowered, tears streamed down his face.

Judas priest! Emmett watched in fascination. *What an actor! What a politician! He's ready for prime time! For the first time in my life, I got a break! What a pity that cameras weren't allowed 'cause every woman in this country would've wanted to comfort him. This guy is great. He could be president!*

Chapter 11

Aunt Rose strolled to campaign headquarters, the storefront on Third Avenue, several blocks from her brownstone. As she approached, she was handed an *OUR WAY* leaflet by a volunteer.

She looked at Way Hampton's picture and thought, *He certainly is handsome... a far cry from Emmett.* Posters of his smiling face were plastered all over the neighborhood stores and shops. Aunt Rose peered through the window and saw her nephew surrounded by people of all ages and backgrounds. He seemed lively and animated, his eyes glittering as he spoke to the volunteers, giving them a pep talk.

She tugged at the heavy door but couldn't budge it until a young man came to her aid. Emmett was so engrossed he didn't even notice her.

"Give us your time and your loyalty. We can win with your help. I see it!" He raised his hand and looked off into the distance like a TV evangelist. "We will take over this third-world town and bring civilization back. New York is no longer the center of the world. We're the butt of jokes. Turn on the night shows, and you'll hear them. Way Hampton promises to bring back love and harmony to this lost empire. Give him a chance. It means your very survival. Now, let's go! Go out there and get those signatures. Then go out there and get the vote!"

A cheer rose as they clapped their hands in unison, chanting, "Way! Way! Way! Way!"

Aunt Rose saw a changed man, alive and invigorated. *He looks just like his father. Too bad he didn't take after Ellen!* She thought about her pretty younger sister who was disowned and disinherited for marrying "the Greek." Her father called him that. What hold did Nicholas Phillippi have on her for her to defy her parents in that way? Something bonded her to him.

Aunt Rose watched the lean, five-feet-six-inch frame, the hawk-like nose, high cheekbones, and small dark eyes, thinking that he was a copy of his father. The only thing missing were the liver spots, like chocolate chips, which had dotted the older man's face in later years.

Yes, there were many similarities, she thought, *even down to marrying Martine, another beautiful woman.* She couldn't figure out that one either.

#

Signatures were piling up to put Way Hampton's name on the primary ballot. He had the backing of conservative groups, but he was also making inroads with some women's groups, a symbiotic phenomenon.

The front-runner of the Republican Party was becoming alarmed at Mr. Hampton's popularity, and even many of the prochoice groups allowed Mr. Hampton to debate with them. He was never testy, always pleasant, even when he disagreed. Some women were quite taken by him. He had the "every man's appeal" of a Jimmy Stewart, and he charmed his way out of some nasty confrontations with feminist groups. Emmett kept Lily Hampton at bay, feeling it was better to keep the wife in the background. She didn't appreciate this and was developing a hatred.

Some feminists were hostile and humorless, but the public sense of fair play played in the hands of Way Hampton.

"It's not a life," they screamed. "It's just a clump of tissue."

"You're right," he replied calmly. "But those tissues have fingers and toes and the form of a tiny baby. By the way, I look around this audience and see so many attractive, healthy-looking, and... smart women!" He stabbed the air with his finger, punctuating every word. "Why aren't you passing your DNA on to the next generation? We have plenty of fools in the world. Why are you intent on destroying a generation, kids with good genes, kids who just might be able to do something worthwhile for humanity? Remember, population growth isn't a threat. Population decline is the challenge. What happens when fewer babies are born so there won't be enough workers to sustain the economy, let alone support the elderly?"

One feminist poked her friend and joked, "I don't really fall for that, but if he knocked me up, I might think twice about getting rid of it."

"He is good-looking," her friend replied. "I vehemently disagree with him, but I don't dislike him."

#

As Waverly gained popularity, Clark Wilkens, the Republican front-runner, truly became alarmed. The third candidate was no threat; the only threat was Way Hampton. If he got on the primary ballot, he may not win, but he would take away votes.

Wilkens called an emergency meeting at his campaign headquarters in the Rosemont Hotel. They occupied several large offices on the second floor. The hotel, which had been elegant in its heyday, had never been renovated and was now dated. Worn carpeting and overstuffed furniture smelling old and stale in the lobby and cocktail lounge were symbolic of the drab, dreary atmosphere of the hotel. The rooms weren't any better. But its cheap rates and centralized location in midtown Manhattan made it a convenient place to stay for foreigners on low-budget packaged tours.

The Wilkens camp happened to be here because it was the Republican headquarters in New York, which was leased on an annual basis, and they liked the cheap rent. They were certain that Wilkens would get the nod until Way Hampton came along.

"Have you seen the *Post* today?" Wilkens asked his campaign manager during a meeting of his top aides. "They've taken a straw poll to see if Waverly Hampton would have any effect on us in the primaries. The answer was yes. He would come out being a spoiler. He would take conservative blocks of voters away from us, diluting our chances of winning. Do something! For God's sake, do something! Can't you pin that murder on him? I swear he had something to do with it."

"It wouldn't wash," came the reply. "There was absolutely nothing to tie him to that murder. You have to be very careful of a libel suit."

But Wilkens continued, "Maybe that slimy campaign manager hired some old hag to do it. You're not going to tell me they were thrilled to adopt that kid!"

"Clark, I'm advising you to be careful what you say. You're starting to sound desperate. The parents were stopping the adoption proceedings, so what would they gain?"

He sat there in silent frustration. "Did they know about the retraction?"

"I can't tell you that," his aide explained, "but Phillippi was exerting a lot of media pressure on the parents. He was relentless, and it worked. They'd had enough bad press and made the retraction, so you must be careful with your accusations. Lighten up and have a sense of humor, Clark. It's the Democrats you have to worry about. As far as our primary goes, you'll be the winner."

Wilkens pointed a finger at him and narrowed his eyes threateningly. "If I'm not, it's your ass I'm gonna skewer. Right now I'm worried about the primaries *and* Way Hampton. I'm not taking any chances. Dig up some dirt! His wife's a dog, so he's probably screwing around. He's so nice," he spoke sarcastically, moving his head from side to side, fluttering his eyelashes.

"You think he's gay?" an adviser asked.

"Who knows?" Wilkens answered. "He's gotta be into something. S&M, drugs, guys, whores. Find something!"

He grabbed his briefcase and started to leave the room when an aide called after him, "Shall we hire a private detective?"

Clark popped his head back into the doorway. "Now you're talking." With that, he left, leaving his aides to find some way to stop Waverly Hampton.

"I know a guy at Moe Deets Agency," one of them ventured. "I heard Krauss does a good job."

"Yeah, but they're not cheap, and they do mostly security work."

"Nah," another man interrupted. "All agencies do grunt work."

"We need a bloodhound."

"Johnny Peester's Company, JP Associates. He's a former cop and has a few bloodhounds on his payroll."

"Let's try them. If it doesn't work, we'll get someone else."

They made the call, and the next day, Rocco Prevetti was hired out of JP Associates.

#

Rocco was a beefy man in his early fifties, stocky and muscular, a fireplug of a man. The fabric of his well-cut suit strained against his forty-eight-inch shoulders, and the holster he wore underneath didn't help. He looked formidable, but he was courteous and well-spoken. He met with the committee questioning them about any lead or gossip they might have heard about Waverly. But they had nothing.

Rocco got to work immediately, putting Waverly under surveillance for several days, and his contact with the phone company supplied him with Waverly's phone records. There was no indication of drug use. There was nothing linking Waverly to illicit sex. Rocco called campaign headquarters, pretending to be with the Board of Elections, and got the name of Waverly's accountant. He bluffed his way with the accountant, checking for tax fraud.

He came up empty, all in one week. Finally, Clark Wilkens met with him privately. The next day, he traveled upstate to Watertown, New York, Waverly's hometown, and spoke to old neighbors, teachers, former classmates, and teammates, saying he was doing a story on the candidate. All he ever got was that the guy was as good as he looked. Rocco visited the local college library, poked around the 1975 yearbook, and read the college newsletter. That's where he got his first lead: "Congratulations to Laura Evers and Waverly Hampton on their recent engagement. We wish them the best life has to offer."

This was the January 1985 newsletter, six months before graduation. Obviously, a lot of changes took place in those six months because Hampton didn't marry this woman.

Rocco stealthily tore the girl's picture out of the yearbook and began to track her down. She was probably married and using another name. He didn't expect to find anything: people break off engagements all the time.

When he entered the administrator's office at the college and leaned on the counter showing his badge, the women instantly became attentive and helpful. This was something out of the ordinary, and it broke up their monotonous routine.

51

"This young lady, Laura Evers, was willed a sum of money by an elderly aunt who lost touch with the family."

The women were so excited they almost drove him to her house, which was in another town about one and a half hours away.

"Mrs. Bartell—that's her name now. She always sends a check to the alumni fund," one of them said. Then she laughed and added, "Maybe with the inheritance, she'll send a bigger one!" He thanked them for their help then drove to her home. After a few wrong turns, he found the small gray Cape Cod with white trim in a middle-class neighborhood. There were planters on the porch filled with colorful blooms, and the small lawn was neatly manicured.

He got out of the car and quickly looked around, hoping not to draw the neighbors' attention. He heard no kids, so he assumed they were indoors or there wasn't any around. He climbed the brick steps and rang the bell. There was no answer. He rang again and waited, but still no one came. He looked in the picture window. The room he saw was more comfortable than elegant. It was neat—too neat. He saw no signs of anyone, not even a pet.

He looked at his watch. *Five thirty. I'll wait awhile in the car. She must not be home from work yet.* He went down the steps, hurried to his car, and backed up until he was in front of her neighbor's house. There he waited until a dark-gray Taurus pulled into the driveway.

She's driving an old car, so she's not doin' that well.

A slim brunette got out, carrying several packages. She climbed the steps, put the key in the lock, and went inside.

She's alone. Good, he thought.

He was out of the car and ringing her doorbell before she had a chance to remove her jacket. She opened the door, and he flashed a badge, asking if he could come in.

"No" was her curt reply. "What do you want?"

Hmmm, she's gonna be harder than the college dames.

They spoke through the jalousie.

"Mrs. Bartell—"

"Miss," she corrected him.

He noted a hint of bitterness. He pulled out a blank paper and looked at it. "I have a Mrs. Bartell written on this. My apologies."

"I'm divorced. Now, what's this all about?"

"Waverly Hampton—"

"Waverly Hampton!" She slammed the door in his face.

Wow! He hadn't expected that. *She either loyal or hostile. I'll choose the latter.* He pressed the doorbell with no success. As he stood there, he went over the facts in his head.

They were engaged to be married but obviously didn't. She was divorced, so that relationship went south, and the speed with which she corrected Mrs. was a dead giveaway that she was very bitter. A woman alone, speaking to a strange man, would want him to think there was a man around but not Ms. Bartell. She hated men, and Rocco Prevetti was there to find out why.

He left the porch, certain that her curious eyes were following him. He drove to town and, after a decent dinner, checked into a local motel and set his travel alarm for 6:00 a.m. He wanted to be there early. If he missed her, it might mean another night in this burgh, which was something he didn't need.

After watching TV, he fell asleep and woke refreshed at six. By seven, he was parked near enough to the house to spot her but far enough away not to be noticed. He munched on a bran muffin and washed it down with lukewarm coffee.

Before long, his bladder was making him think about the porta-potty, but he hesitated to use it. *Don't take a chance, Rocco. If you lose her, it's another day lost.*

By eight fifteen, he couldn't hold it anymore. He unbuckled his belt, unzipped his fly, and relieved himself. As he reached the comfort zone, he saw her leave her house and hop into her car. Rocco stopped quickly and set the potty down the second he saw her turn toward him. He ducked down and lay across the seat until he heard the swoosh of the passing car.

He popped up quickly and made a U-turn, thankful that the potty didn't overturn. Unbelted and unzipped, he took off after her, feeling the cool morning air on his genitals. He tailed her about fifteen minutes.

Her car swerved into the driveway of the Old Pine Manor, a square box of a building about five stories high. Lines of rectangle windows broke the monotony of the beige bricks. A pine tree shielded the front, ominously close on a stormy day, but it added a freshness to the stark building with its deep-green color.

What is this? A motel? Or a catering hall? The sign gave no indication of what the manor was.

Laura Evers Bartell swung into a slot on the employees' side and slipped into a side door, setting off an alarm. Rocco heard the piercing screech as he parked and thought better of doing that. He would use the main entrance. He felt the cool air below and zipped his fly.

Leaving the car, he walked around to the front lobby. He swung open the door and almost tripped over a dozen old people who were sitting around, staring into space or nodding off. Walkers, canes, and wheelchairs were strewn all over; and he had to carefully pick his way over the cheap thinly stretched carpeting, his heavy frame bouncing the floor beneath with every step. The place had the lardy smell of old flesh; and he caught a whiff of urine as he finally reached the front desk, catching his foot on the leg of a walker and dragging it along a foot or two before replacing it in front of a dozing man.

"Christ, looks like Lourdes," he said to the pretty young thing behind the desk, wondering if she ever heard of it. "You've heard of Lourdes?" he said. "Oh, sure, Madonna's kid." The town didn't seem big enough to have such a large elderly population. He looked her over as she stepped around to pick up a fallen cane. She wore a tight black skirt, which was glued to her hips. When she bent over, it hiked up, showing most of her thigh. Her shapely legs were covered with flesh-colored stockings. The contrast was startling.

She walked back to the desk and looked up at him with huge green eyes rimmed in black mascara. Stars and half moons dangled from her ears, almost hidden by the mass of long curly titian hair. The pink gloss on her lips made them shimmer as she opened them slightly, waiting. A tiny plaque above her left breast said her name was Holly.

He leaned forward to be closer. "I need some information, Holly. I need a nursing home for my mom. She's ninety."

"God bless her," said the pretty young thing, "but this isn't a nursing home. It's a senior residence, and a very good one, I might add. We have a nurse and a beauty parlor on the premises. The rooms are plain, but people from all over want to get in. It's reasonable, and the help is honest. But there is a waiting list."

"How long?" He watched her glistening lips and felt like moving in himself. Rocco had a taste for young women.

"A few months." She leaned forward, and he smelled her clean breath and the musk she wore. He glanced at her cleavage and knew he wouldn't mind spending his old age here. "They either get deathly ill and are transferred to a nursing home, or they just die. Hospitals don't want them." She whispered, "That's the only way we get vacancies. After you speak to Laura Bartell, our administrator, I'll show you around. Then I'll put your mother's name on the list."

Laura Bartell... bingo! he thought.

"Her office is through there." She pointed to a hallway. "First door. Just walk in. We're very informal."

As he turned to leave, he saw an old man stop breathing, then watched in fascination until the old guy sputtered, honked, and started to breathe again. He turned to the girl. "How can you stand this, a lively young girl like you?"

"We're having an Alzheimer's Day. It happens every so often, when they all seem to fall apart at once—it's catchy!"

"Don't you find it depressing?"

"Sometimes, but I have lots of boyfriends to cheer me up." She lowered her voice. "I need lots of sex to keep my feet on the ground." She giggled, and Rocco Prevetti, private eye, knew who his dinner companion would be tonight.

"How about dinner? We'll talk about my mom."

"Sure," she answered. "See me on your way out after you talk to Laura, but don't tell her about dinner."

"I won't. It'll be our secret."

"By the way, is Amy Bartell her daughter?" He made up the name.

"No, she has no kids."

"Okay, see you later, sweetheart." He walked down a corridor and made his way to the administrator's office and knocked.

"Come in."

Laura Bartell wasn't pleased to see him. "What the hell is this?"

"Look, I'm here for one reason," and he blurted out quickly. "I'm only trying to find out what kind of man Waverly Hampton is."

"A rat, a louse!"

"Because he broke off your engagement?"

She didn't answer.

He sat down in the chair opposite her and recited, "You loved him. He left you. You married on the rebound. Now you're divorced, alone, and working in this joint."

"I'm working in this joint because there are not a lot of jobs around here. We have become the dumping ground for old people, but it does provide jobs, and I'm grateful to have one." She opened her desk drawer and took out a cigarette. "We're not supposed to smoke, but you're pissing me off. So I'll take my chances."

He picked up the matchbook, leaned over, and lit it, noticing her trembling hand. "And you need a cigarette because of me. Hey, I'm not that bad. I'll be very straight with you. My client, who is in politics, would like to discredit your old boyfriend. He'll really make it worth your while."

"I have nothing to say. There is nothing more." Her hand went to her blouse, and she fingered a small gold cross hidden beneath her lapel. He was relieved to see the cross. She was Catholic, so maybe there was a kid somewhere. "What happened to me happens all the time between people. There's no deep dark secret. He wasn't ready for marriage, that's all."

"No deep dark secret, hmmm?"

"No," she answered too quickly, and he knew she was lying.

"Okay, then I'm outta here. Thanks for your time." He rose, and she said nothing more.

He stopped at the desk to confirm his dinner date and then drove back to his motel. He called New York and reported his findings, but he still felt there was something she left out. He was in the business a long time, and you develop a sixth sense about people and their behavior. His sixth sense was telling him that she was lying. Maybe there was an illegitimate child somewhere. She was Catholic, and if there was a kid and she gave it up for adoption, he would have to find that out. If he could prove it, Mr. Clean would be dead in the water.

I'll stick around another day, ask around, get into her house, try to find some pictures. They could tell a story. I wanted to get back to New York, but I guess I'm stuck with Holly. He grinned to himself, looking forward to an evening with the supple young woman. And suddenly he wasn't so eager to leave. He remembered his employer's words. "Stay as long as you need but find something. Otherwise, we'll have to resort to dirty tricks to stall his train. Waverly Hampton and Emmett Phillippi must be stopped. I didn't come this far and work this hard to be derailed by two very devious, ambitious men. If you can't find anything up there, resort to dirty tricks, but don't tell me about them. I don't want to know."

Hmm, Rocco thought, *dirty tricks could be more lucrative then this boring work. Okay, I'll have my date tonight, then leave.*

Chapter 12

Kiwi was taking particular care with her appearance, especially on days Emmett dropped by campaign headquarters. It wasn't far from Aunt Rose's, so he always made a point to visit her and remove some valuable trinket, always with Martine's approval. It was for the cause.

Winsome began noticing things were missing or out of place, and she immediately blamed Kiwi and company. She confronted the homeless woman, "You white bitch, you takin' things on that nice old lady after what she's done for you and that pack of scum!"

"I... I... I never took nothin', an' neither did Harry."

"*Someone* is. You think I'm stupid 'cause I'm black? I see lots of things missin', and you better bring 'em back!"

"Winnie, you think I would be so dumb? We would be the first people you'd blame, an' we got it good here. I ain't gonna screw that up. An' if I tell Harry what you—"

Winsome bumped her with her plump body, pushing her off balance. "You threatening me, crackhead bitch? If you are, I know people who would slit your throat for a buck, so don't make me laugh with the skinny-ass Harry!"

They eyeballed each other, but Kiwi said nothing more. She would protect Emmett to the end, and he would be grateful and fall in love with her. She left immediately and went to campaign headquarters to find Emmett. She drew him to a private corner, tugging at his sleeves.

He pulled away and spoke to her with disdain, "What do you want now? What are you stammering about?"

"W... W... Winsome knows things are missing, an' she's blaming me."

"She's probably right. Why are you telling me this?"

"I saw you take them."

He was immediately on the defensive. "You saw nothing, liar!"

She was crushed by his harshness, never really expecting that. She thought they would be co-conspirators, working together and living together. She would get rid of the others. But now he admitted nothing, and instead, he was shifting the blame to her. It wasn't going the way she had planned.

"I... I... I saw you take the jade the night she gave you the big check. I didn't say nothing. I could've ratted you out, but I didn't. All I ever did was help you."

"I don't need your help." He waved her hands away, turning up his nose in disgust. "Get away from me before you give me fleas."

She couldn't believe he was so mean. She had bathed at Aunt Rose's and borrowed her cologne, and she knew she didn't smell. "You think I'm stupid? Well, I know about you." She felt braver now. She would show him she was no dummy to be treated like dirt. "You didn't give the street people their money. I know you kept it. So if I were you, I wouldn't be so rotten. I know a lot about you, and I'll tell your aunt, and then where will you be?"

She wanted to curse, but she bit her tongue. She had to keep herself in check; it was too soon to reveal that side of her. Perhaps he would come around, see her in a different light, and take her off the street.

From the other side of the room, Harry watched with interest. Kiwi was his woman, and he knew she was upset; he could tell by her facial expressions and body movements. Lately, she talked much too much about Emmett, making excuses when he welshed on his promise to pay the street people. He got them to sign, using phony IDs and addresses. He then told them the money hadn't come through yet when he, in fact, cashed the check.

As Harry watched them in conversation, he saw hurt and admiration in her face, and he knew Kiwi was smitten with this ugly old man. A jealous rage started to engulf him. He imagined an affair. Were they having a lovers' quarrel? He didn't want to lose her: she was valuable to him. It was she who had befriended Aunt Rose, making their lives better. Watching them together in deep conversation, he wanted to smash Emmett's ugly face. He stormed over menacingly and pulled Kiwi by the arm.

"Stop makin' an asshole of yourself." Then he turned his wrath Emmett, who was startled. "Leave her alone, you ugly fuck."

"I have every intention of leaving her alone," Emmett said indignantly. "Tell her to leave me alone."

"You heard him. He's not interested in you. He'll never marry you and take you off the street. Stop dreaming! He'll just use you for sex."

"Sex?" Emmett protested in shock. "You belong in a loony bin! I don't know which of you is crazier!" He glared at her so fiercely it almost inflicted pain. He lowered his voice, and venomous spittle sprayed through his teeth. "I want you to know that I was married to a great lady—a great lady! I've built a shrine to her in my heart. I would never sully her memory by having intimate relations with the likes of you!"

There was a rapid-fire blinking as tears poured out of her eyes. Devastated, Kiwi suddenly doubled over with pain. The disappointment of her dream was like a kick in the stomach. She covered her face with both hands, and snot trickled out of her nose. The volunteers watched in fascination, not knowing what to think. Her plan hadn't worked, and he had embarrassed her. Perspiration glowed on her face. Her bangs hung like spider legs, dangling over her forehead in damp clumps. She felt hot and clammy and smelled like a wet dog.

But the two men ignored her, intent on discrediting each other, spitting at each other like a pair of tomcats.

"Now you know what a jerk he is," Harry said triumphantly, pulling up his lean frame and looking down at Emmett, his florid face creased in anger. "You ugly bastard, you crook, you cheat!"

"Stop it! Stop it, Harry!" Kiwi grabbed his arm. *He'll spoil everything,* she thought. She was making headway with Emmett, and Harry was spoiling everything.

"Stay away from her, or I'll screw you up for good."

"She's yours," Emmett said magnanimously. *I gotta get rid of them,* he thought. *Pay them off to leave the area or set them up for a drug bust, but I got to get rid of them.* He had to do something! Harry was loose cannon. He would think about it later and choose the best plan, but now there was work to be done.

It was exactly at this minute that they secured the 7,500 signatures on the petition. Wild cheers went up from all the volunteers, and the unpleasantness of five minutes ago was forgotten in the carnival atmosphere. People threw papers in the air and hugged and kissed one another.

Emmett left the homeless pair to make a call to the media and to Waverly Hampton. Volunteers ran to the liquor store to buy chilled New York State champagne, and they toasted the fruits of their labor with plastic glasses. Waverly Hampton rushed to join them. Press and TV crews interviewed the happy crowd while Harry looked ominously at Emmett. Then he grabbed Kiwi's arm and strode out into the daylight, away from his hated rival.

"We'll tell the old lady, Kiwi. We'll fix him," Harry took charge.

"What if she doesn't believe us?"

"She will. She knows her nephew. Then he'll be out, and we'll be in. Then me and you, we'll get hitched, an' we'll look after the old lady."

"You mean it, Harry?" Kiwi looked pathetically at this scarecrow of a man, who finally had his own dream.

"Yeah, honey, I mean it." He put his arm around her to show his love.

#

Way Hampton's rival, Clark Wilkens, received the news with regret. "They made the deadline by the skin of their teeth, those lucky bastards."

59

The private eye hadn't been able to dig up anything. He'd tried to track down an illegitimate child by grilling his young sex pistol for information about her administrator; but she could tell him nothing, except that Laura didn't date and seemed to have no interest in men, never talked about her private life.

"Maybe we're looking at the wrong person," said Clark Wilkens. "Check out Mrs. Hampton. It would be great if they were a gay couple, married in name only." A desperate Wilkens was grasping at straws.

A town meeting was scheduled with the three Republican primary candidates. And Clark Wilkens needed something to discredit his rivals.

But in the Hampton camp, they rolled up their sleeves, and Emmett trained his man like a parrot, with an answer for every conceivable question. He had to stay on a roll, and nobody would stop him because this was his last chance to be somebody.

Chapter 13

Aunt Rose was furious. Why did he have to spoil things? Now the store would have to be put on hold. If she had been there, she wouldn't have allowed this to happen.

"Did you make goo-goo eyes at Kiwi, leading her on?" she demanded.

"Never! How could you ask that? Is everybody insane?" an incredulous Emmett asked the wall he was facing.

"I know men."

"Well, you don't know me if you think I would go for her." He was losing his cool. If his aunt turned on him or if Harry complained to the Board of Elections, all would be lost. "Never, never, NEVER did I lead her on. She fantasized everything. She offered me sex! Can you imagine? Sex!"

"Isn't that what people do?" she replied, unflappable.

"Not with her." There was sincerity in his voice. "I have no interest in her at all. I did not invite any of this. I did not instigate anything. She's an obsessive nut, and if your tattlers lied, then it was just to get back at me."

"Why, Emmett?" Her voice was sweetly accusing. "Why would they want to get back at you?"

"I don't know. Maybe they're jealous of our relationship."

"Jealous of us?"

"Yes. If I'm out of the way, they would just take over, and as you age, you'd lean on them more and more. They know what they're doing."

She sighed. "All this talk is tiring. I'm sick of it. You still spoiled everything." She shot him another barrage as her eyes closed a minute. She was old and tired and had enough for one day. But Kiwi was expected, and she wanted to be there for the promised payoff to make sure Emmett kept his word. He would pay them to leave the city. Perhaps they could get a fresh start somewhere, but she was exhausted, and she finally dragged her old body off the chair and up the stairs, resting every two or three steps. It was like mountain climbing, every step a challenge. She collapsed on top of her quilt and was in deep slumber, softly snoring within seconds.

Emmett was glad. She would only interfere, so he allowed her the rest she needed.

When Kiwi arrived, the atmosphere was strained. He was polite but reserved, not wanting to send the wrong signals and go back to square one. He made it very clear that Harry wasn't welcome; he would only deal with Kiwi.

She searched his face for any signs of softening.

"This will only take a minute," he said curtly. "Then I hope this is the end of it! Do I have your word?"

"Yes. I only wanted to be friends with you." She made a last attempt. "I don't see why—"

"Don't start," he sternly said.

She followed him into the kitchen, which was good enough for her. The second he left, she spotted the liquor on the table and was dying for a drink. Her hand trembled as she reached for it, opened it, and took a big swallow, then another, and another. The sweet amber liquid was comforting.

Emmett stood framed in the doorway, watching in disgust. *Thank god, I'll be rid of that vermin after today,* he thought as he entered, handing her the envelope. She wiped her mouth with the back of her hand and said nothing, reaching for the envelope.

"Make sure Harry gets his. I trust you'll keep your mouths shut. Otherwise, I'll resort to other measures. This meeting is over."

#

Several hours later, a refreshed Aunt Rose trundled downstairs. "Did I miss Kiwi?"

"She was gone in a flash, only interested in the cash. That's the end of your business venture."

"I hope you were fair with them."

"I was more than fair." He shook his head wisely.

"Good." The old lady was pleased. "Perhaps the two of them will go off into the sunset and leave me alone. Maybe they'll go to Malibu. They're looking for homeless people in Malibu." He laughed. "For the first time in my life, I'm that close to the golden ring!" He held his thumb and forefinger a hairbreadth apart. "This time next year, I could be running New York City, and then I'll show you just how brilliant I am. Don't let me down, Aunt Ro."

He kneeled in front of her, wearing his shiny suit. A closer look at this shirt revealed a frayed collar, the broken threads sticking out like insect legs. It brought a pang of pity to her heart.

"We only have each other, Aunt Ro, and I want you to be proud of me."

Suddenly, she felt old and useless. Everything hurt. Her feet, her back, her hip—perhaps it would rain. That always made her bones ache. "Oh, Emmett, I'm getting so old. At least that foursome made me forget it. I know I couldn't rely on them, but I have fun. You're the only one I can really rely on. Will you take care of me when the time comes?"

He was desperate for money. Why didn't he ask for it now when she was so vulnerable? *After all, it is rightfully mine. My mother's share went to Aunt Rose. It's rightfully mine.* But he just said, "Yes, Aunt Ro, I will always take care of you, but you must also take care of me."

"You are well taken care of, Emmett. You're my sole heir."

It was the first time she had ever said that, and he was relieved to know he would inherit everything. He would now give her more attention. He was resentful but would play the game.

#

Aunt Rose missed her friends! With campaign headquarters nearby, Emmett took her there on occasions, but he also came by regularly to check up on her. He was busy planning the great debate, so he did a lot of the work at the brownstone and kept her company. He also wanted to be certain the homeless were out of their hair, not sneaking around somewhere. He told Aunt Rose that he had given Kiwi the money to buy their silence about the phony signatures. He said nothing about the missing objects.

She seemed depressed not having those simple souls around; somehow she felt they were decent in spite of what everyone said about them. She was on the outs with Millicent and now looked forward to Tuesdays and Fridays when Winsome cleaned. Some days she felt weak and shaky. She hadn't felt that way before, and it all started when Emmett began hanging around. *He's making me nervous with his silly campaign,* she told herself. *I'll just go get a checkup, get something to make me feel better.*

When Emmett learned of her plan, he quickly offered to accompany her. "You can't go alone."

"But you're so busy with the campaign. I'll go alone."

"No, I'll check my schedule and make the appointment for you."

He never did, and she wasn't feeling any better. She actually felt worse, finally taking matters into her own hands.

The hell with Emmett! Next thing I know, he'll be putting me away in some nursing home. I need my independence, and Emmett is becoming over solicitous, getting on my nerves. He might even assign a volunteer to accompany me, and I don't want some stooge hanging around me. So she made the appointment and with the help of her cane went alone. *Afterward I'll go to the park to look for Kiwi. Emmett must have scared the living daylights out of her.*

She sat in the doctor's office in a stark waiting room, with seats lining the wall and magazines in crooked piles on the tables. She looked around at all the vacant elderly faces and counted her blessings. So far, she had her health, financial independence, and Emmett. *Such as he is. I truly hope he makes it this time! I've had enough of these schemes.*

"Rose Parsons." The nurse broke her reverie. She eased herself out of her chair and followed the nurse.

Her doctor took blood and urine samples and was concerned about her rapid heartbeat, so he took an EKG. She got a thorough going-over, but no medication would be prescribed until all the results were in. The aches and pains came with old age.

She began to feel good, getting out of the house and outsmarting Emmett. She would take her time getting home. *To hell with cabs. Knocks me out just getting in and out of them.* She walked with confidence to the bus stop. The cane was great! It was support, a companion, and a weapon. *Why didn't I think of it before?* With this in hand, she was formidable. A bus came along, and the driver lowered the steps. It was a struggle to get on board, but she did it.

As the bus neared Thirty-Fifth Street, she pressed the button and rose from one of the front seats reserved for the elderly. The bus pulled into the stop. The doors opened. She teetered for a second, afraid to step down, and looked at the driver, who seemed preoccupied. He had forgotten to lower the steps.

She banged her cane loudly, shaking him out of his reverie. "Lower those fucking steps," she yelled. She was suddenly shocked at her words, but a ripple of laughter went through the bus. Nobody seemed offended, not even the driver. Her face turned red; and she lowered her eyes, keeping them fastened on the steps, daring not to look up. She was relieved to hear the whirr as they were lowered. She clambered down, embarrassed to the core. As the bus pulled from the curb, she quickly peeked up at the smiling faces looking at Mrs. Santa Clause with a cane, saying the *F* word.

Oh, what the hell, she said cheerfully. *I learned something from my friends, and it worked! He lowered the steps!*

She hobbled to the park, thinking about all the things happening around her. Emmett was riding a wave, and for the first time in his life, it looked as though he would make it. She muttered to herself as she walked. *Good! Maybe he'll be so busy he'll forget about me. I don't want him dictating to me. I'm not senile. He's the one who messed up with Kiwi and ruined the plans for the homeless store. I can't for the life of me figure out what she saw in him to disrupt everything and make Harry jealous. But I do hope they learned something from me.*

She walked past her door and continued to St. Andrews Park on the next block. It was a postage-stamp-sized neighborhood park that no longer heard the delight and laughter of children playing. It served as a toilet, hotel, and shooting gallery for homeless drug users who lived in boxes along the FDR Drive. Animal droppings littered the pathways. Perhaps Kiwi would be there, afraid to contact her because of Emmett's wrath. Perhaps someone would know where she was.

As she approached the entrance, she saw several police cars parked every which way. *I wonder why they're here, rounding up the homeless,* she thought. *Maybe the cops know of Kiwi's whereabouts!* A man was lying on a bench, and several police were around him. The park seemed deserted, the homeless scattering like roaches when they heard the sirens, but this guy stayed put. She hobbled over and looked at him. He was an African American in tattered clothes.

"What's the matter with him, Officer? I know him. He's a fixture in this neighborhood."

The policeman looked at her with interest. "Do you know his name, ma'am?"

"Yes! Henry... Henry," she struggled with her thoughts. "White—that's it, Henry White."

"Easy enough," the cop responded. "Blacks are called white, and whites are called black. Figure it out, why doncha?"

"I haven't seen him around lately. Is he sick?"

"No, ma'am, he's dead. We're waiting for EMS. This is the second death of a homeless this week."

"Who was the other?" she quickly asked. "Was it a woman?"

"No, another guy, a white guy."

"Was his name Harry?"

"I dunno, ma'am. There was no ID. The medical examiner said it was drug related. I wonder if this'll be the same."

"I would be interested in knowing about this man. He was part of a group I tried to help. Can I call you, Officer?"

"Sure." He scribbled his number and handed it to her.

"Thank you, Officer." She ambled out of the park and went straight home, dyin' to call Winsome. It has been an exhausting day, but she felt good in spite of poor Henry's demise. It felt good to be independent again.

Chapter 14

The three potential candidates were ready for a face-off. Clark Wilkens, the favorite, knew who his enemy was, and it wasn't Dorfman. This debate was scheduled, but the party leaders would be a tough, dragged-down fistfight, and the winner would represent the party on the ballot. They expected the worst.

The men mingled, shaking hands and working the powerful crowd. Emmett made certain Waverly was well versed on everything. Clark Wilkens could be a scrappy fighter when cornered, so they had an answer to every conceivable question. There would be no surprises for him and no alcohol. Emmett forbade drinking on such occasions, so Waverly drank plain water in a "dirty" glass, which was the way he described his drink. If he wowed the crowd, he could win the primaries—a long shot.

The political leaders wanted to hitch their wagons to a winner. Suddenly a voice came over the sound system along with the ever-present screeching and whistling sounds. They finally adjusted it, telling the audience to be seated. The debate would begin, and the orderly crowd holding notebooks and pens took seats.

The three men were seated on the dais, with Mr. Wilkens in the middle. A pad, pen, glass, and water pitcher were in front of each man. A young girl sat directly in front of the dais with a stopwatch and a yellow sheet of paper, which she would hold up when their time was up, allowing a few minutes to each man.

A question was read; and they answered in turn about business, taxes, unemployment, and crime. Waverly expressed his views like an economist, remembering on cue everything Emmett had taught him. He was well versed, impressive, and held his own better than his rivals. Dorfman was teetering. You could tell by the audience's reaction that they were less interested in what he had to say.

But the group was peppered with prochoice representatives from women's groups who were very interested in the abortion issue since these women could not risk ever having *Roe v. Wade* overturned. So they were interested in hearing how Mr. Hampton would handle this.

"Mr. Hampton," the female moderator said, "do you believe that sex education should be taught in the schools?"

"I'll probably sound old-fashioned, but I believe in the three Rs," Waverly said. "Without them, you can't work or support yourself. We have the highest dropout rate in the nation and the highest illiteracy rate right here in New York. When I hear some of our kids speak, I don't understand them. Everything sounds foreign to me, and yet they're Americans speaking English. They only express themselves in vulgarities and obscenities, and that saddens me. How can these children ever get decent jobs and work in the mainstream?" The yellow paper flashed, but he continued, "Why can't Johnny read? Because he doesn't get a chance to read! He's too busy learning to put condoms on cucumbers instead of learning the three Rs."

The applause was deafening.

"Mr. Wilkens," same question.

"I think our friend here is right... for a New York thirty years ago. But he's a little out of touch with reality." Emmett scowled at him. "The fact is that young people, some as young as twelve and thirteen, are engaging in sexual activity. This is alarmingly much younger than their counterparts of twenty years ago. So we have to deal in facts and reality. Teaching sex education, taking the ignorance out of sex, just might prevent unwanted pregnancies and the spread of AIDS, as well as other diseases. Kids as young as twelve and thirteen are having babies. You can keep your head in the sand or you can face facts, and the fact is that kids are having sex. The rate of out-of-wedlock births is an alarming 45 percent, about 136,000 a year, and most go on welfare. So how can we turn this around? Families play a large part in it. So don't you think we should try to educate them? The kids and the families."

Waverly jumped in. "We are, and look what's happening. It's not working! So preach abstinence. Give that a try."

"Get real, Waverly." Wilkens was bullying him.

"What's wrong with self-control?"

"It's not realistic in this day and age."

"Maybe it should be."

"You're right. It should be, but this is the real world, not the fantasy work you live in," Wilkens replied.

The girl kept flashing the yellow sheet. It was the third man's turn to talk, but he got lost in the popularity of these two men who were so opposed to each other. Emmett caught his man's eye and signaled him to go for the jugular, baiting him.

"Mr. Wilkens, you're upset because I'm doing well. A lot of the party's votes will be cast for me regardless of the fact that I'm Protect Life. This is a crippling aspect to a candidate, especially in New York, but I'm not afraid to wander out of the politically correct lanes. I'm unapologetic about that, and I'm still popular and gaining."

"That's 'cause you have a good PR machine. What you're really trying to do is impose your will on women, taking us back to the turn of the country! Abortion is between a woman, her doctor, and God. If it is morally wrong, then she's got to answer to God, not to you. It's not illegal in this country, so I believe we should all abide by the laws of the land!"

He got a thunderous applause as he sipped water and nodded to the audience.

"Clark, there's no argument here," Waverly smoothly replied. "I agree. We have to abide by the laws of the land. I'll even accept the draconian RICO law, which was intended to deal with organized crime but is now applied to those who block abortion clinics. I don't like it, but I'll accept it. Earlier you spoke of the quality of life, and this is what I'm aiming for. I believe that starts in your heart."

"It does," Wilkens answered. "But each individual in this country has the right to determine their bodily functions without threats or physical interference by religious or special interest groups or politicians such as yourself, who condone murdering doctors over a blob of tissue." His voice rose. "How can someone claiming to cherish life can then deliberately murder someone?"

Waverly answered in a calm, controlled voice, thrilled that Wilkens was becoming emotional. "I agree with you again. But I'm afraid you're the one out of touch with reality about prenatal life. It's hardly a mystery. You call it a blob of tissue. During the first month, little limb buds appear, and these grow into arms and legs. And by the twentieth day, the heart starts to beat. Clark, your blob of tissue has a heartbeat. A heartbeat!"

"Mr. Hampton, have you ever fathered a child?"

A murmur rippled through the audience at the personal question.

Waverly knew Wilkens was fishing, but he suddenly felt hot. "No, have you?"

"You know I have children."

"And I do not. Perhaps that's why I'm so passionate about life."

"Mr. Hampton, does the problem rest with you or your wife?" Wilkens was suddenly very formal.

A groan went through the audience. This debate was getting too personal, and Emmett wasn't prepared for this one. But Way answered quickly, "It rests with me."

Emmett leaned back with relief. *Good boy, Way. I taught you well.* When the audience stood up and applauded, he rose too, pleased that the embarrassing question was dirty pool and the crowd resented it. Wilkens was trying to make Way sweat, but all they got was a public admission of sterility, which Emmett knew nothing about.

The private eye sat there, taking it all in. *Shit, there goes the illegitimate-kid theory. He can't father a flea.*

As the debate continued, Emmett mulled the admission of sterility over in his mind. *I didn't know, but perhaps it's good. Nobody can slap a paternity suit on him in the middle of the election. Yessiree, it may work to our benefit.*

"You right-to-lifers," the third man spoke up, "are not kind, gentle people. You're a pack of wild dogs bent on scare tactics. You've murdered because you can't stand anyone thinking differently. You're intolerant! If you have so much concern for life, why don't you just adopt some of the unwanted kids? There are plenty of unwanted, abused children around. Why don't you put your money where your mouth is and do something for them?"

"I did," Waverly pointed out. "I was willing to adopt an unwanted baby."

"But he was conveniently murdered," Clark Wilkens quickly added.

Shock waves went through the crowd. This man was coming off as a mean-spirited, nasty old man, and he was losing the audience with his low blow.

"Yes, he was. This case is still open, and I pray every day that the murderer will be found and brought to justice just as I hope the murderers of doctors at abortion clinics will be brought to justice. I cannot and do not condone any of those actions. I am prolife!"

There was a long loud applause. The girl held up the yellow sheet for their final remarks.

Clark Wilkens had a polite response, but Waverly was clearly the winner. He was on a roll.

"I'll end by saying that it is obvious that the ultimate example of disrespect for life is a mother killing her unborn defenseless child. It has a ripple effect, and we all become desensitized. If a nation tells a society that a mother has 'the right' to destroy the living child within her, then why are we surprised at a society gone mad? I rest my case."

The applause was deafening. It had been a two-person race. The third man never left the gate. But Wilkens and Hampton were neck to neck, almost a dead heat until Wilkens forgot the rules of decency. Now Waverly Hampton, a gentleman throughout, was the winner.

"I don't think I'd vote for him, but I do respect him. He is fine," one woman said.

"Do you think he's sterile?"

"That's right up my alley," said one prochoice woman. "Sterile doesn't mean impotent. And he's got to be one of the best-looking men around." She looked longingly at the candidate standing among well-wishers.

Emmett was jubilant! *Sweetheart, we're on our way,* he told Martine, knowing she would be proud of him. His man had wiped out the competition. *Thank you, thank you,* he whispered to no one in particular.

The party bigs surrounded Waverly, who charmed them as well as the press. Wilkens and his men watched with envy from the sidelines: the handshakes and

69

back patting, the thumbs-up, and the toasts! Sparks of hatred crackled as Wilkens locked eyes with a triumphant Emmett. *He still has the look of a loser,* he thought. *Everyone is vulnerable somehow. Way Hampton has to have an Achilles' heel. We just haven't found it. We've got to dig up something, and we've got to do it fast! If he doesn't get the Republican nod, he'll run on the conservative line. I'm sure of that. Any way he runs, he's a spoiler, taking votes away from me.*

"Find something," he commanded his men. "Find something fast."

Chapter 15

Winsome carefully mopped around the old lady's bed. Aunt Rose wasn't well.

"Ms. Rose, it ain't like you to take to your bed. You sure someone around here ain't doin' somethin' funny?" she asked suspiciously.

"The tests showed nothing abnormal, Winny," the old lady replied.

"I don't believe in tests," the feisty woman asserted. "I believe in my gut. I would just keep an eye on what I ate or drank around here."

"You prepare the food, Winny."

"I do, but I ain't around when you're eatin' it."

"I'm just older and weaker."

"Just like that." Winsome snapped her fingers.

"After all the fun and games, I'm paying the price. It's been weeks since I saw Kiwi and the boys. They just disappeared, never even came by to say good-bye," She was clearly disappointed.

"He's playin' with fire, Ms. Rose. Every time they need money, they gonna show up on this doorstep. It could go on for years. Addicts kin never git enough money."

"And what about that Henry, dying in the park? It's all so sad, Winny. I really liked them and tried to help. They made me feel young. Now I feel so old and decrepit," Aunt Rose said.

"Ms. Millicent say—"

"You still call her that?"

"That's what I calls her. I ain't callin' her some fancy new name. It's Millicent, 'takes it or leaves it,' I said, or her house cleaner is gone, and that's that. Well, she said they jumped the back fence coupla days ago. Late one night when she couldn't sleep, she's walkin' from window to window, and she swears she saw that Harry digging in the garden on his knees, foolin' around on the ground. You know what I think? I think they took things from you, buried them in the garden 'til they were ready to split. There's lotsa things missing around here. They stole 'em for a new start. That's why they never came around to say good-bye to you, that white trash. After what you did for them!"

"Emmett gave the money to get rid of them. Winny, could you give me a drink?"

Winsome placed her mop against the wall and poured a glass of water for the old woman, who drank slowly.

"That's better. I get so thirsty. As much as I like them, I couldn't have them threatening Emmett." She lowered her voice, her eyes widened with confidentiality. "Harry threatened him, you know, because Kiwi was smitten. Can you believe that? That poor girl having a crush on Emmett? I can't imagine anyone having a crush on Emmett."

"I heard all about it, and so did Ms. Millicent, who thought Kiwi had a nerve overstepping her bounds, and she blamed you. After all, she said, 'Mr. Emmett's not a homeless man.'"

"He would be if it wasn't for me, and when I die, he will inherit what I have. It's not a fortune but nothing to sneeze at. You see, the trust my father made, leaves everything to charity—his favorite hospitals and foundations. The house will be sold. The painting and valuables will go to the Met. In spite of all my reasoning, he wouldn't listen. Just a stubborn old man who held a lifetime grudge. He despised Emmett's father. The Greek, he used to call him. He disinherited Emmett's mother."

Winsome's eyes flew open, intrigued by this family's clash of wills.

"And when I die," Aunt Rose continued, "it all stops. Emmett gets nothing from that trust."

Being a practical woman, Winsome asked, "Does he know this?"

"No."

"Well, I think you better tell 'im fast, Ms. Rose." A grave concern came over her. "It ain't like you to suddenly take to your bed, getting weak."

"Oh, Winny, do you really think he would do me in?"

"Hmmm." She shook her head from side to side, mulling it over. "People do funny things outta desperation. I think you better tell him, an' I think you better tell him fast."

"In time. Now, don't worry." She leaned over and squeezed Winsome's hand. "As long as I'm alive, there's a considerable income rolling in." She screwed her face in thought. "You know, Winny, it wouldn't be a bad idea if he hooked up with Millicent when I'm gone. She's older, but she would provide a place to live and financial security." But Winsome gave her a disapproving look. "Ms. Rose, I know your nephew ain't no beauty queen, but that Millicent sure is a faded old-looking maid." She rose to dust a little. "You told me she had a secret. Was a man involved?"

72

"Oh yes," the bedridden women replied, taking another sip. Winsome, who loved gossip, spun around, pulled up a chair, and eagerly waited for more.

These two women, who were worlds apart, had a deep affection that was truer than being kin. They expected nothing from each other, and that made the friendship genuine. Beneath all the polite "Ms. Rose" talk, they were real friends. The gossip was therapy for the old lady, who took another sip of water, then began, "I was a newlywed. We had lived in this house about a year, and her father, Dr. Foster, was always polite but aloof. Millicent craved friendship, and she would come over to tea and liked having a younger woman in the neighborhood. Her mother had died, so all she had was this nasty German maid who I think, though I never thought of it before, was sleeping with or doing something to Dr. Foster. She had a lot of power in that house, and she watched Millicent like a hawk. She was paid to do that.

"A young-looking repairman came to fix their air conditioner. They were the first in the neighborhood to have one. He came several times, and Millicent was in love. She was so starved for attention she fell in love with any man who was nice to her. Her domineering father felt that nobody was good enough, but that was just a ploy to keep her there. He was mean-spirited, telling her they only liked her for her money. Besides, she had graduated from NYU, and this guy was just a repairman.

"She sobbed, saying it wasn't so, that this was true love. So Dr. Foster cunningly invited the young man over while he made Millicent listen through the door. He offered him money to go away, and the man accepted. It was a mean and heartless thing to do to a young girl. That selfish old man. She was devastated, rang my bell, and sobbed in my arms. But the kicker was he never paid the boy."

Aunt Rose was starting to feel better relating this story to such a good audience. Winsome sat there mesmerized peeking into the private life of the dull spinster next door.

"Dr. Foster twisted the story around, saying the young man was out to get money, but Millicent felt he loved her. She told me he came back the next day begging for forgiveness, saying her father intimidated him, and she forgave him on the spot. Before she quite knew what was happening, they were in bed together."

"Millicent in bed with a man?" The incredulous woman was wide-eyed. "You mean they did it?"

"Yes! But the German spy—and I'm sure she was that—called Dr. Foster immediately, and he left his office in a rage, leaving his patients stranded. He quietly entered the house, tiptoed upstairs, and caught the young couple in flagrante delicto."

"What that mean?"

"Doing it."

Winsome laughed. "Ms. Rose, you sure have a way."

"He yanked him out of bed and threw him down the stairs, yelling. The whole neighborhood heard it. I called the police, fearing a murder, and there was one. I'm sure of it. Dr. Foster ran after him and pushed the boy, and he fell against the marble mantle and struck his head. Millicent lay there naked and in shock while the others quickly dressed the boy. When the police arrived, Foster told them the man broke in and tried to rape Millicent. He lied, and Millicent said nothing! That one never did have any gumption."

"You mean the boy died?" Winsome was popeyed.

"Yep, and Millicent's been odd ever since. But Daddy always took care of her. Even in death, she lives on a handsome trust fund."

"Can't picture it, her havin' sex. Did they really do it?"

"I believe so." She winked knowingly at Winsome, who was cleaning in fits and starts, more interested in the story than in dusting. "At one point, she looked very heavy and stayed indoors a lot."

"You sayin' she done get a baby?"

"I'm not saying she did or didn't, but I have my suspicions. Remember, her father was a doctor, and after the war, the German spy went back to the fatherland a very rich woman. And my husband saw someone in the garden one night."

"You sayin' they killed the baby?"

"That, or she might have had an abortion. They were very strange people."

"She said she was never with a man." She started to polish the furniture.

"That's what she wants us to think. I also know another secret. There is something dangerous in her garden. My husband found out."

They felt a draft as the front door opened, and they heard footsteps in the foyer, then on the stairs.

"Aunt Rose?" he called up.

"Up here, Mr. Emmett."

"Does he know?" Winsome quickly asked.

"We'll talk later."

"How's my best girl?" He seemed a little too cheerful.

"Not bad. Winsome is good medicine for me."

"If you don't feel better, we'll get the doctor."

"I'm okay. But nobody's seen Kiwi and the boys. Do you know where they went? Henry up and died in the park."

"I heard." Emmett shrugged. "Guess the others took off. That was the deal, wasn't it?"

"Without saying good-bye to me. It's strange they never came by."

"You never learn, Aunt Ro. They were the dregs of society. I'm surprised you're still alive."

"He's right, Ms. Rose. They was scum."

"I've worked so hard to get my candidate to this point. I couldn't risk having a delusionary woman and her jealous boyfriend making up stories, threatening me."

"Threatening you? I thought it was a love triangle."

"That too, but it was the signatures. He threatened to expose that." Emmett shook a finger at her. "Now don't play Ms. Innocence. You knew all about the signatures. You were very pleased when Kiwi came up with the idea."

The old woman looked sheepishly at Winsome. "He's right. I knew."

"My lips are sealed, Ms. Rose. Ain't notin' new! Politicians been buyin' the vote in Harlem for years. I made a buck or two myself."

"Well, it wasn't right."

"Don't matter what's right or wrong to politicians. It's winnin' that counts."

"I'm relieved you understand. But I still want to know where Kiwi and the boys went. North, south, east, or west."

"Why don't you just drop it, Aunt Rose? Who cares where they are?"

"They's probably just down on Twenty-Third Street 'til they run out of money," Winsome added.

"We should get the locks changed," Emmett advised.

"That ain't a bad idea, Mr. Emmett. We sure don't want some crazed crack addict coming in and harming Ms. Rose."

"No," he said emphatically, "no, we do not!"

Chapter 16

It was dusk. The old woman, kerchief covering her head, looked like Queen Elizabeth at Balmoral Castle on a rainy day. She walked slowly and heavily down the park's pathway, dragging her shopping bag. It was a colorful plastic bag. There weren't any neighborhood people taking the sun. Occasionally, some brave senior citizens would band together and try to recapture the park, but they were forced away by the foul language and fear of violence. Most of the toughs lived in boxes along the FDR Drive. Aunt Rose was glad none of her people were considered dangerous, and she had been making headway with them when everything collapsed.

Several homeless men were sprawled out on the benches that lined the walkway about every thirty feet. They were newly painted green and looked clean and glossy. One of the men took out a knife and began etching his initials in the new paint. Another man was lying down, his hands cupped behind his head, using them as a pillow. One leg dangled off the bench. He opened his eyes and watched his friend.

"What the fuck you doing? You want the cops to come down on us? We have a good spot, so don't screw it up."

"Aaahh, shaddup. You don't know what a good spot is. I had a good spot with the old lady up the street. She fed us and gave us money, and we hung out in her house."

"G'wan. Nobody's gonna do that."

The third man piped up, "He did. He had it made!"

"Yeah," Harry continued, "Then that ugly fuckface screwed us. I'd like to kill that bastard."

"Ain't seen you around lately," one of them said to Harry.

"I been in detox. I took some shit. Next thing I knew I was in Bellevue, sick as a dog, almost died. When I get out, my woman's gone with a wad of money, half of it mine. She just took off. Couldn't wait for me, probably took off with some fuckin' crackhead! Nobody knows."

"That's whores for you. Never met one you could trust. They forget you like that." He snapped his fingers.

The third one was quiet, taking it all in.

"Me and Billy stay on the drive, but the heat's on, and the city's gonna put us out. That's the rumors, anyway."

"I'm gonna get my hands on some cash soon, maybe get a place, I dunno. I need the cash, though, and I know where to get it from that cheatin' bastard. And if I don't get it, that tight ass is gonna be the sorriest man alive. Nah, I won't kill him. I'll do something worse. I'll fuck up his mayor campaign."

"Yeah, sure you can," the man answered, unimpressed.

The men suddenly took notice of the figure walking slowly toward them. They looked at her with curiosity and wondered why she wasn't afraid of them. Everybody else was; yet she sat down on a nearby bench, leaned over, took out a banana, and peeled it with great ceremony, carefully removing the fragile strings clinging to it. She put all the garbage in her bag, then slowly ate the banana, savoring each bite.

The men continued their chatter, but she was not intimidated.

One spoke loudly, "A black guy dropped dead here last week."

"Cops all over the place."

"No shit. I just got out two days ago. I gotta get some cash." He looked toward the old woman, who was enjoying her fruit. "You got some money for us, Grandma?" he yelled.

"A little," she answered and dug into her coat pocket and tossed some change into the air toward them. The sun caught the shiny coins falling like sparkling confetti. The men lunged off their benches, making a dive to pick it up. Before they said another word, she reached into her shopping bag and pulled out a brown paper bag. "I have something better."

They moved toward her and grabbed the bag out of her hand, recognizing the shape. All three hungrily pulled at it as the woman shook her head in disgust. *No manners, not even a thank you,* she thought as she picked up her shopping bag.

They couldn't wait to tear off the brown paper revealing the bottle. The tallest man held it high while the others leaped and grasped at it. He teased them. "Kentucky bourbon," he tantalized them.

"I'll drink rotgut. Gimme some." When he had his fun, the tall one drank, then passed it to the others.

The three men drank thirstily from the bottle, taking turns to die. When they were quiet, she picked up the bag and bottle and walked slowly up the pathway out of the park.

The next morning, neighbors walking their dogs called the police. Two homeless men had been found dead in the park within two weeks. All died from toxic poisoning in their alcohol. "It is possible that there's some rotgut somebody's selling or were they murdered," the ME's office wondered. And today, three men died in the park together, comrades to the end.

Harry was one of them. The kind old lady did Emmett a favor.

Chapter 17

"That was very noble of you!" Lily Hampton's voice dripped with sarcasm, clashing with the gentle colors of the room. The sun-washed walls gave just a hint of yellow. She tossed her Fendi bag onto the seafoam-green silk chair and kicked off her shoes, standing in stocking feet on the lush mint-green Chinese rug, which dominated the room. "Did you feel you had to protect me? Is there a stigma to being childless?"

"No, of course not." He was astonished. "It was a very personal question coming from a boor. It was none of his business."

"Why didn't you just say that?"

"Because this was better. It did him in. People thought it was dirty pool, and he's running scared."

"Good, you got what you wanted, Way. Would you have married me if you knew I was barren?"

"Yes, of course, I love you!" he answered irritably, then changed his tone. "Look around you. We're living in a Monet painting." He thrust his arm out, taking in the quiet surroundings. Pastel watercolors decorated the walls. Fragile vases were placed about. "You have exquisite taste in everything, especially men." He laughed.

She didn't join him. She knew he was meeting young attractive women. Her long brunette hair, which had looked good eighteen years ago, did nothing for her now. Now it was just long stringy gray hair. She looked like an aging debutante. Her cultivated speech seemed affected when she mingled with ordinary people. Her expensive clothes looked dowdy compared to other women, who were more easygoing in their manner as well as their clothes, and she saw the disappointment on their faces when she was introduced. She could almost read their thoughts. *He married her?* All told, she was no beauty queen.

"I'm very comfortable with you and our marriage," he said. "I love our life. You're willing to take a backseat and let me be the star. I love the attention. I'm eating it up. Hey, I'm a Leo! We love attention."

"I know. I've lived with you for eighteen years. But we're getting older. Doesn't it bother you that we have no kids? Your DNA is not being passed on," she continued her sarcasm.

"We almost had a child, remember? And we were lucky to have gotten out of that one," he spoke honestly. "It doesn't bother me and don't get any ideas like Janet Husking did. That was absolutely tragic. Emmett told me they're divorcing. The marriage couldn't withstand all the blows. She should have left well enough along. I always wondered if there was something more to it, if they were involved in that murder. I could never understand why anyone would want to kill that poor unfortunate thing."

"Well, whoever it was, they did us a favor!" Lily answered. A dark side to her personality was emerging, brought on by her jealousy. Occasionally, she allowed a glimpse but then backed away from her ugly thoughts. Lately, though, she found herself surrendering to it, insecure with her handsome husband. "I still think Emmett was behind the whole thing," she continued. "I don't trust him."

"Emmett hired someone? Come on, he's not that stupid. Lily, if there's one person you can trust, it's Emmett. You don't like him, that's all, but Emmett is so hungry for success he hadn't made one misstep. He's shooting for the stars, and I think we're gonna make it, thanks to him. He could see Lily wasn't happy with his choice of words, but it was true. When she ran the campaign, it was for want of something to do, as a hobby. Emmett was a professional. He thought of everything. Emmett came up with a wild idea that just might appeal to the masses. Adopting unwanted American babies. He waited for her reaction, but he drew a blank. He swears it will catch on and snowball across the country. If I get elected, we might have to adopt a token baby, put our money where our mouth is."

Her eyes widened in horror. "A minute ago you told me to forget about kids."

"This is only if I get the Republican nod," he assured her. "It might be a smart move if we decide to enter national politics."

"Now it's national, I'm not thrilled with that."

She's being a pain again, he thought. *Here I am at success's door, and she's being contrary.*

"I resent him for telling me to keep my distance from you at political rallies," she complained. "Why does he do that?"

"I don't know, but there must be a reason. He's got sound judgment."

"I'm surprised you haven't figured it out because I have. He wants you to appeal to the women who regard you as an enemy. Without me around, you're free to charm and flirt with them, win them over."

"It's working, isn't it? They say I have the primary in my pocket. Wilkens can run as an independent, but I've got the Republican and conservative endorsements. They haven't announced it yet, but it's in the bag."

"All at my expense! I won't be treated like I don't exist." Her voice became shrill. "I won't be pushed aside by some ferret face who barged into our lives with empty promises."

"They're not empty. He has us reaching our goal."

She's jealous, he thought.

"It's *your* goal! I can't stand the sight of lovesick women fawning over you. How many keys and phone numbers have you collected so far?"

"Please, Lily." He walked away in feigned disgust, knowing that he had a matinee with one of the beautiful prochoice women. It was the second time he took a chance and got away with it, ducking his entourage with an excuse of a much-needed nap before the evening's events. The raunchy sex seemed to invigorate him, and he shone at these fund-raisers.

"Answer me, how many?" she shrieked after him.

He turned to face her and in a calm, distinct voice said, "None. I'm not interested in anyone but you!"

She glared at him, not believing a word as he tried in vain to reason with her.

"They treat me with respect, Lily. I'm not a sex symbol. I'm a father figure."

"Not anymore. Not since you cavalierly announced to the world that you're sterile. A very convenient means of birth control." Hurt showed in her face. He had never seen her like this, an insecure wife locked in on her fantasy. "There will be open season on you with your 'built-in protection.' Every woman will want to screw you!"

He grabbed her shoulders and gently shook. "Stop it! Stop it, Lily! I thought you wanted to help me. You helped me before."

"That was fun. It made me interesting. It gave me something to talk about. Now, I'm just in the way, pushed aside by that obnoxious little gnome. You don't need me anymore. You need Emmett! Why can't it be the way it was, before Mr. Phillippi took over our lives with his schemes? And look what he has come up with. Adopting babies? Then what? Am I supposed to slit my throat?"

Her hands covered her face as tears flooded her eyes and heart-wrenching sobs heaved her body. She wanted comfort and reassurance, but the phone conveniently rang; and Waverly left to answer it, getting away from this emotional scene. He continued talking at length while Lily waited. *Perhaps I was being childish. I'll wait and apologize,* she thought, hoping he would come to hold and reassure her.

She waited well over an hour as he talked with Emmett, planning their assault on the public's sympathy using the babies. He knew she was upset, and once again, he chose Emmett. *Why didn't he call him back? What could they be talking about for over an hour? Maybe it's a woman. Maybe he lied to me.* She went into another room and quietly picked up the receiver but heard Emmett's voice.

"Is someone on the line?" he asked gruffly.

"Yes, I am," she admitted. "Waverly, I want to speak to you."

"In a moment, dear. This is important."

She hung up, muttering, "And I'm not. Our marriage is reduced to this, living in the same house and communicating by phone."

She went into their bedroom, hoping he would come in. After a while, she heard the muffled sound of the television news in the den. It confirmed her fears, and she cried herself to sleep.

Chapter 18

BABYTOWN, USA, the headline screamed from the front page of the *Post*. GIVE US YOUR TIRED, YOUR POOR, YOUR KIDS, the *Daily News* winked. And the "Old Gray Lady" ran a story on page 3.

IF ELECTED MAYOR OF NEW YORK, WAVERLY HAMPTON, WHO IS GAINING SUPPORT IN THE REPUBLICAN PARTY, HAS SAID HE WOULD APPEAL TO CITIZENS ACROSS THE NATION TO ADOPT UNWANTED CHILDREN.
"TAKE THEM OFF OF THE STREETS, OUT OF POVERTY. TAKE THEM INTO YOUR LIVES AND YOUR HEARTS. AND I APPEAL TO ALL WOMEN NOT TO DESTROY LIFE. HAVE YOUR BABIES, AND WE WILL TAKE CARE OF THEM. GOD WILL HELP US FIND A WAY. HELP ME MAKE BABYTOWN, USA, A REALITY."
"IT WAS AN EMOTIONAL APPEAL THAT GARNERED GREAT INTEREST AND SUPPORT," MR. HAMPTON'S CAMPAIGN MANAGER SAID.

#

"The guy's nuts!" Clark Wilkens ranted. "They're both nuts!"

"Delusionary," corrected his campaign manager. "His platform is based on fantasy. He got the idea for this craziness at the debate. Remember when Dorfman asked why he didn't adopt an unwanted child? Now they're exploiting it."

He was right. It was exactly when Emmett got the idea—while he was sitting there at the debate, listening. His computer mind took it all in, throwing out most of it; but when Dorfman asked the question, it clicked.

"Babytown—why not? There's Boystown for unwanted boys, so why not a place for unwanted babies?" The wheels turned, and it made sense. It had appeal.

How could anyone turn their back on a baby—on this idea? You can't go wrong with kids or animals.

The next day, Emmett scheduled a photo session at the Foundling Hospital. He was running with the idea and taking it as far as it would go. They sat Way Hampton in a rocking chair surrounded by babies and a few cuddly kittens. There were babies on his lap, in his arms, and at his feet. One little guy, back to the camera, was climbing onto his shoulder, and toddlers on unsteady legs were holding on to him for support. Some were sitting at his feet; and a very cute baby face was peering over his right shoulder facing the camera, a hidden volunteer holding her. It was a blockbuster. Way had the charisma of a John F. Kennedy, and when that picture appeared, he was neck to neck with his rival.

When asked to comment, Wilkens replied, "People love fantasy. I call this fantasyland."

"Is Boystown a fantasy?" came the Hampton rebuttal, and the public had to admit that it wasn't. "Every idea starts as a seed of fantasy. I see it—Clark Wilkens does not. I'm a visionary. He is not. So you tell me. Who would you like to represent you: the same political hacks or someone with vision?"

It was a harsh statement for Waverly to make, but Emmett had become a pit bull. He had taken an unknown a scant eight weeks ago; and today, that man had the attention of the political bosses, steamrolling to capture the candidacy. Nothing must spoil the momentum.

And as much as Way enjoyed his time in the sun, it was marred by Lily's jealousy. She hated everything: the flirting, the publicity, the sex-symbol label. And to compound matters, he began receiving calls and letters from admirers. They were certain Wilkens was behind them.

"It comes with the territory," Emmett said with a shrug. "Anyone with celebrity status is vulnerable, so consider yourself a celebrity, and don't worry."

But he did worry. He didn't want anyone compromising his candidate. He began to accompany the younger man everywhere, and Waverly had to nip his new affair in the bud. Fortunately, she understood and would wait it out. He accompanied him to his hair stylist, the tailor, his club, where Emmett decided he must discontinue the massages.

"Never put yourself in a position where some male or female can claim you made a pass at them. Look at what happened to Clinton!"

He ordered a pulsating showerhead that massaged Way's body while he showered at home. The hot claps of water stung his flesh, but Emmett thought it was safer than human hands near his genitals.

He made peace with Lily, allowing her to be visible, scheduling her to talk at senior citizen group meetings in the boroughs. He wanted harmony, and she did well with the old folks.

It was at one of these meetings that a blue-collar type accosted her. He was a toothless old man, his pinched mouth opening and closing like a bellows, puffs of air surrounding his words.

"I know your husband from way back. He went out with my niece. Promised to marry her. She didn't think too much of him."

"I'm sorry to hear that. I think a great deal of him." Lily was uncomfortable and tried to walk away, but he persisted.

"He married you, dumped her. Let the bygones be bygones. You gotta number? She might wanna talk to him after all these years, say hello. They were upstate, in college together."

"I'm sure he'd be happy to hear from her, but we have an unlisted number. I'm sure you can understand why. What is your niece's name?"

"Laura. Tell him Laura said hello."

"I will," she replied then moved on to speak to others but was shaken by this pushy old man. On the ride back to Manhattan, she thought about what he'd said. Way never mentioned a Laura. And when she relayed the message, she watched him closely. He stiffened a bit but quickly regained his composure.

"Laura, Laura... Gee, I forgot about her. Someone I dated in college."

"He said you were going to marry her."

"Maybe that's what she thought, but it wasn't on my mind."

Perhaps, Lily thought. *But he was not pleased to hear her name. I wonder why. Maybe they still see each other when she comes to New York.*

She was becoming irrational.

Chapter 19

When Rocco Prevetti left upstate, he realized he had never used a condom. Too late now, he reflected, as the monotonous thruway zipped past exit after exit, bringing him closer to New York City. He stopped to get gas and used the men's room and paid by credit card. He looked for his notebook to jot down the charges but couldn't find it.

Shit. He looked through his pockets, between the seats, placing his hand into the upholstery, checking the floor. *I hope I didn't lose it. I have everything in it. I might've left it at her apartment. It's gotta be there.*

He quickly called the manor on his cellular phone, and Holly was happy to hear his voice, cheerfully announcing what a great time she had. But, no, she hadn't seen the book. "If I do find it, I'll mail it to you. Give me your address."

He hung up disappointed. He'd have to recreate his expense account. He was equally disappointed that she had only asked his address for the lost item. She really wasn't interested in him.

#

Holly left her desk and went directly to Laura's office, leaning seductively against the doorjamb, waving the little black book she held between her thumb and forefinger.

"Look what I have." Laura looked up. "You might be interested in reading this. Your name appears all over the place, and you were right. He's a private eye. Never told me. Still insisted he had the old mother, right to the last kiss."

"You're incorrigible."

"Well, I think you should see it before I send it back," she said. She handed the book to Laura, who thumbed through it, reading his notes. She spotted Way Hampton's number and address and jotted them down. "Are you involved in something?" the young woman asked.

"No, not at all. They were just checking on someone from my past."

"Good, I thought you might be in some kind of trouble. Let's go to a movie sometime."

Laura hesitated. She resisted being chummy with her employees. But Holly seemed so vulnerable in spite of her cheerfulness and her many male friends. This sleeping around with guys she barely knew was unhealthy. Laura wondered if she was ever sexually abused, bent on a course of self-destruction. *Maybe I can save her from herself,* she thought.

"Okay, Holly. How about Friday night?"

"Sorry, gotta date on Friday." She winked at Laura.

"Then you let me know, and I'll be here to pick up the pieces when they rip out your soul." She thumbed through the book. "This is interesting. I'll return it later."

"On second thought, just toss it. I'll never see him again."

After Holly had gone, Laura read page after page carefully. These people were looking for something. After Rocco spoke to her at the manor, he had broken into her house, knowing she was at work. He was looking for something to discredit Way Hampton; it was all written in his notebook.

A creepy feeling came over her, knowing a stranger had been in her house going through everything, and she didn't even sense it. *How did he get in? Pick the lock? Open a window?* She visualized him going through her closets and drawers, sneaking quietly from room to room, looking at family pictures, opening her refrigerator, knowing what she ate and drank. He probably looked in her medicine cabinet, knew she was constipated, knew she had allergies, knew she was depressed, knew she no longer had a period. He saw her bed and her nightie; perhaps he touched it.

Chills ran through her. She put the book in the drawer and pulled out a magazine telling the story of Way Hampton's incredible rise from obscurity. She stared at the handsome face. Then she lit a forbidden cigarette and puffed furiously, building up her anger against this man; and while she stared at him, she began to formulate a plan. A plan that would destroy her old love forever.

Chapter 20

Blessed silence! The candidate finally had a morning to himself—it was a rare treat these days. A generous backer had a business emergency, so the luncheon date was changed. Waverly had the luxury of a free morning. There would be no reporters, no photographers, no Emmett, no Lily who went to Saks to choose some "stumping" outfits. Waverly had encouraged her to see a fashion consultant.

A strategy meeting was penciled in at 2:00 p.m. Emmett always made good use of time. But until then, Waverly would lie in bed, drink his coffee, and read the *Wall Street Journal*. He would use his shower massage. He laughed at Emmett, not trusting the masseur with his private parts anymore, always looking for ways to prevent scandal. Perhaps he was right, he would see his new sex partner after he became mayor.

So Waverly lay in bed, stroking his penis and thinking of her. He needed sex. It would help him unwind, and sex with Lily was becoming a thing of the past with their busy schedules and the total exhaustion at the end of the day. They should have done it before she left, but she turned him off with her jealous outbursts.

He let his mind wander to an erotic scene, and his testicles began to feel scratchy. It felt good. Sex on the desk at Gracie Mansion—why not? Kennedy did it on the Oval Office desk, and so did Clinton. He saw the scene, but Lily wasn't in it. It was the new woman. Then the phone rang and broke the mood.

Dammit. He rolled over to answer but decided to let the machine pick up.

"Way, this is Laura Evers Bartell, a voice from your past. I have to speak to you. Call me at area code..." and she gave the number. "Call me. It's important." The voice was commanding.

He sat up, no longer interested in sex. This was a big surprise, and he was shaken by it. A voice from your past, she had said. But he had forgotten about her; people block out unpleasant memories. He pressed the replay button and heard the message again.

What the hell does she want after twenty years? He reached for a pen and jotted down her number but thought better of calling her. Suppose she taped the conversation? Suppose she tricked him into saying something incriminating? He would ignore it and play it safe. If Lily heard it, he would pretend it was that kook from the senior center who said his niece knew Way.

It disturbed him, though, and he began to worry. Maybe he should say something to Emmett. He would know what to do. So Way's free morning turned into another phone meeting.

"Emmett, I had a call from a woman I dated in college years ago."

"What'd she want?"

"I don't know. She left her name and number."

"Is it somebody you were involved with?"

"We were engaged, and I broke it off."

"Nothing more?"

"No."

"Can she use anything against you?"

"Hey, you know the saying, 'If you want to beat a dog, you can always find a stick.'"

"Then ignore it," Emmett advised. "How did she get your number?"

"I don't know."

"I smell Wilkens," the suspicious man said. "He put her up to it. It reeks of Wilkens. He'll stop at nothing."

"He's almost as bad as we are." Waverly laughed.

"Not quite." Emmett joined him, enjoying the camaraderie and his role as the successful promoter. Waverly depended solely on his judgment.

"All right, Emmett, I'll ignore her. I hope it's the end of it."

It wasn't. Several days later, the registered letter arrived at campaign headquarters. It was addressed to him, but Emmett signed for it and read it:

Dear, Way,

You're a bad boy for not returning my call! It's been awhile. How many years? I've seen you on TV, and I read about your incredible rise in politics. You're doing well. But I can't for the life of me understand your platform. How can a man run on a prolife platform who arranged an abortion for his pregnant fiancée in some back-alley kitchen? Where, if you remember, I went into shock, almost bled to death, and ended up in a hospital—alone. I could never have children, a factor in my divorce. How could a man like this run on a prolife platform?

I remember your phone call breaking off with me, the coward's way out. I remember you sneaking off to the big city to pursue your career, leaving me a physical and emotional mess. How can such a man speak of values when he has none?

You're still taking care of number one. I can't ever forgive what you did to me, and I will not allow you to fool the public. I need compensation for what you did, and if I don't hear from you within forty-eight hours, I will go to the media with my story.

Laura Bartell

Her telephone number was printed neatly under her signature.

Emmett stared at the letter, his hand trembling. He began to feel warm and clammy and fumbled with the knot on his tie, trying to loosen it.

It could be a kook, but it had a ring of truth to it. He couldn't be certain until he talked to his man. But Waverly swore there was nothing incriminating in his past.

Just three days ago, he assured me there was nothing to it. He just broke off an engagement. Now she's accusing him of vile things. Please, please say they're not true, he spoke aloud, hearing the words, trying to sort it out. *Martine, he asked his wife, "what could be the worst of it? Blackmail? We could cope with that.*

If this woman wanted money, he'd have to confront Aunt Rose and demand his share of the family inheritance. She was an old lady, so what did she need it for, anyway? Waverly would have to kick in too. There wasn't much time. She'd given him forty-eight hours to contact her, and Emmett was a nut cluster of desperation, mopping the perspiration from his brow.

What a mess! I didn't expect this. I never expected this. I'd better call her immediately, not let her wait. I can't take the chance. He yelled out from his office to the volunteer manning the switchboard, "Hold my calls." He locked the door, picked up the phone, and dialed. The phone rang several times, and then someone answered, "Laura Bartell?"

"Yes."

"Emmett Phillippi, Waverly Hampton's campaign manager."

"Doing damage control, Mr. Phillippi?"

He didn't reply to that but got right to the point. "I just received your letter. Way hasn't seen it, and I haven't spoken to him about it. I don't know who you are, what you are, or if you really know him."

"Believe me, I know him."

"I will verify everything with him."

"And if he denies it, who will you believe?"

"We can always work something out. Whatever you do, don't go to the press. Agreed?"

"Yes... for now. A private detective will contact you in a few days. He will be my intermediary, and we'll take it from there. Thank you for calling." And she hung up.

He sat there, staring malevolently at the receiver. Dammit, she had to drag in a third party. *Maybe she's afraid of conducting the negotiations, afraid of being bumped off.* He smiled as he thought about that, but the smile turned to a scowl. Now he had to confront Waverly and try to keep it between them.

He quickly dialed his number and spoke the instant the phone was picked up. "I thought you were sterile."

There was a long silence. Then Lily Hampton said, "I am."

Hmmm, Waverly is full of surprises! he thought. When Waverly came on the line. Emmett summoned him to campaign headquarters, where they could talk privately.

The handsome man strode in, greeting all the faithful followers who were so eager to work for him. Emmett watched from his office doorway as Way glad-handed his way across the room, chitchatting and greeting one and all. It wasn't unusual for the candidate to come by, and the volunteers loved it, especially the women. One girl flirted openly with him, tilting her head, looking up shyly into his eyes, then tossing her long dark hair in a single sweeping motion.

Waverly stopped to speak to her, returning the copulatory gaze. He enjoyed this, but Emmett didn't. He would keep an eye on her. He was getting anxious waiting for him. *Get on with it,* he thought. *He's taking too long.* He circled the air with his finger like a TV director, motioning him to hurry.

When he finally reached Emmett, they disappeared behind closed doors, speaking quietly in that tiny room. Emmett pulled the chair away from the desk and sat across from him, their knees almost touching. They saw the shadows of the volunteers hovering near the opaque glass, so they would have to speak quietly.

The older man kept his eye on Waverly, tracking his movements. He needed to study his face and his reactions while they discussed their dilemma. It belonged to both of them. If Waverly fell, Emmett would go down with him. He watched carefully with his piercing dark eyes. He knew Waverly well enough to distinguish the slight subtleties in his expression. He knew when he was "on," and if Laura Bartell was lying, he would see it and back his man 100 percent and sue her for slander. The penetrating eyes never left Waverly's face as they conversed in the cramped space, feeling each other's breath.

"Is it true?" Not waiting for an answer, Emmett continued, "If it is, why didn't you tell me? You could have trusted me with the truth." Waverly remained silent. "You never returned her call."

"You advised me not to."

Emmett's voice got louder with exasperation. "You said it was nothing. You assured me there was nothing." He tossed the letter at him. "If I'd known about this, I would have called immediately. You ignored her, and that aggravated the situation. Now it's on paper in a letter, and she must have a copy of this letter. And if this letter gets into the wrong hands—or *any* hands, for that matter—it's the end of us. All my dreams down the drain."

"What about mine?"

"You're young. There's time for you. But it's over for me."

"Emmett, I'm sorry. I didn't think it would come to this. I thought if I ignored her, it would go away, but obviously, it didn't."

"You're saying it's true... all of it?"

The younger man leaned forward with a hypnotic look in his eyes, placing a reassuring hand on Emmett's knee. "We can get out of this. It's my word against hers."

Emmett brushed the hand away, shaking Waverly's confidence. The younger man groped for an explanation and felt a tic in his left eyelid, which was unusual. He hoped Emmett wouldn't notice it, but he did.

"Look, it was a long time ago. We were kids. That's the reason I'm prolife. I made a terrible mistake. Who knew I would marry a woman who couldn't conceive? I destroyed my only child, thinking there would be so many others. But that was it! Unless I divorce Lily, that's it for me."

"That's out of the question now," Emmett shot back. "Political careers are not built on scandal! You know this woman. If we pay her, will that be the end of it, or will she make a career out of blackmailing you?"

"I don't know. I haven't seen her in twenty years. She was sweet when we were engaged."

The stale air in the dry little room began to choke Emmett. He tried to clear his throat but broke into a dry, hacking, nervous cough. Waverly rose to get some water, but Emmett waved him back into the chair, reaching into the desk drawer for a crystal mint. He peeled back the silver-blue wrapper until a tiny crystal-clear donut appeared. He pried the tacky mint free with his thumbnail, popped it into his mouth, and licked his thumb and forefinger, rubbing them together for a quick dry.

"You'll have to kick in," he sputtered. "I can't finance this alone. Can you do it?"

"I suppose I'll have to. I'll sell stock or get a loan from my company. They don't have to know the truth. I need it for the campaign, that's all. Did she tell you the amount?"

"No." The coughing stopped, so he offered a mint to Waverly, who shook his head.

"Not even a ballpark figure?" He displayed a cold clinical attitude at odds with his usual charming nature.

"She gave no hint, just said someone would contact me."

This annoyed the candidate. "Why does she insist on involving a third party? Doesn't she trust us?"

"You answered your own question. It's called being cautious. It's also called a safety measure. I'm afraid, my handsome young friend, that you fooled around with the wrong girl. She's not only bitter. She wants blood. Yours!"

They sat in silence, trying to think of a way to overcome this sudden problem.

"Why weren't you up front with me?" Emmett squinted. His eyes looked smaller than they normally were.

"I was. This is something I'd forgotten about."

"Do you expect me to believe that?"

"All right. If I told you, would you have taken me on?"

"No, and this situation is exactly why. We're being sidetracked. Time, money, and energy are going in the wrong direction. And it's a dangerous direction. One word from her, and we're finished. All the months of planning, the grueling schedule, and the hard work not only by us but by the volunteers. The money. The people who believed in you. You let them all down by lying to me."

"Come on, Emmett." He rose, annoyed, and stood over the seated man. "It was an omission, not a lie. And the public forgives. They forget. I can make them forget."

"What about the sterility question?" Emmett calmly asked. "Is that categorized as an omission or a lie? You announced your sterility two months ago, but the truth is, Lily is the one."

Waverly brushed it off. "That wasn't intentional. It just fell into place that way when Wilkens asked the embarrassing question." He knew Emmett felt slighted by the deceit. He tried to energize the mood with cheerfulness and continued like a cheerleader trying to rouse an unenthusiastic crowd. "Come on, pal, let's concentrate on the blackmail, get the money, pay her off, get it out of the way, and then get on with it." He punched the air with his clenched fist as he'd often seen Emmett do. "We're a formidable team, Emmett."

Emmett watched listlessly without catching the spirit. They were a formidable team, but the blackmail weakened their position. He no longer had the confidence in his candidate, who had not been aboveboard with him. He felt betrayed. Emmett did dishonest things to help the campaign, but he was always straight with Waverly.

Now he looked at him and wondered what else was hidden in Waverly's life.

Chapter 21

Rocco Prevetti was surprised to hear from the woman he had stalked. She left her telephone number on his answering machine, along with a curt message: "This is Laura Bartell. Please call me immediately."

The *immediately* got to him—it was a command. He wondered how she had gotten his number or remembered his name since she had never seen it in print. He had forgotten the missing card case; but he called immediately, and she hired him to be the intermediary at the expense of Clark Wilkens, whom she also contacted.

"I've given this a lot of thought," she said. "I'll get rid of Way Hampton as long as I don't have to meet with him or go to New York, where I might have a convenient accident. As you can see, I don't trust that bunch. So as long as Mr. Wilkens pays your expenses, I'll get rid of Way Hampton for him and for you. Think about it. I'll give you one hour to get back to me with a definite answer. Otherwise, the deal is off."

She hung up, and a feeling of power surged right through to the tips of her limbs. She felt omnipotent. She could change someone's life with a phone call. It felt good. It felt good to have control.

Rocco quickly called Clark Wilkens on his cell, then called Laura within twenty minutes. "It's a go. Wilkens is more than happy to pay my salary, but what do you get out of it?"

"A pound of flesh! I want nothing from Mr. Wilkens. I'll get mine from Way Hampton. Now, here's what I want you to do!" And she explained exactly what she wanted and how he was to negotiate this deal.

#

Emmett and Way scrambled for money. It would take at least a week to raise anything substantial, but Way agreed to sell securities, telling Lily he needed money for the campaign. Aunt Rose was getting weaker and spent a lot of time in bed. She was no longer feisty and depended on her nephew more than ever. He knew she would cooperate.

He sat at her bedside chatting amiably, telling her stories about the campaign, his mind drifting to his current problem as he continued the superficial chatter. He was hard-pressed and could ill afford to play companion to his aunt at such a crucial time, but he needed her help desperately.

"You know, Aunt Ro, we're almost there."

"Good, Emmett. I hope you make it this time. In spite of our differences, you know I truly care about you."

It was the opening he'd been waiting for.

When he leaned forward closer to her face, she saw the pleading eyes and knew it wasn't an act. *He's in some kind of trouble,* she thought.

"Aunt Ro, I need money, a substantial amount. I'm not sure how much—yet."

"Is something wrong, Emmett?"

"Yes, but I can't go into it now. Just say yes. Just say you'll help me. After all, part of that trust is rightfully mine."

She covered his hand with her shaky fingers. "Emmett, there is something I must tell you. I never did before because it would have been worse. You always had hope that one day you would inherit your mother's share. It kept you going. But the truth is, when I die, you'll only inherit everything your uncle and I had. Not a fortune but it's something. Your grandfather's trust owns this house and most of the valuables in it. That's why I never became that attached to them. They will all be sold or donated to a museum. The money from the trust will be distributed to a number of charities, specified by Father. You were left nothing. He was such a bitter man that he took his wrath out on you."

A feeling of angst and dread overcame Emmett, and he felt a tightening in his chest. Beads of perspiration covered his forehead and upper lip. His skin was pale and waxen. He couldn't focus his eyes. He was adrift with nothing in sight, floating alone in a murky sea with nothing around, nothing to grasp onto, his mind on hold. He heard her voice but didn't listen.

"I'm sorry to have to tell you this," she continued.

His breath quickened as he gulped huge whiffs of air, blinking his eyes rapidly to clear his vision. "Can the trust be broken?" he asked when his mind was functioning again.

"I already inquired. It's ironclad. But as long as I live, we will receive the income. Through the year, I have generously shared that with you in your many business ventures, hoping something would take hold."

"And when you die?"

"The trust terminates. The income distributions will cease as soon as I die."

My god, he uttered, feeling lightheaded, breathing rapidly. *She mustn't die. She mustn't die.* He lowered his head, avoiding Aunt Rose's eyes, staring

96

despondently at the floor as resignation slowly settled in. "I should have expected that," he said slowly, shaking his head in disgust and bitterness. "What a bunch. First, my parents left me with nothing but bills."

"They had nothing, Emmett, and I helped."

Anger overcame him. "She should have made up with Grandfather, if only for my sake."

"That would have meant leaving her husband, and that she would never do. Try to understand."

"Oh, I understand, all right!" he barked at his aunt. "All she ever cared about was him. What did she ever do for me? What did either of them ever do for me? Some parents I had. They were so besotted with each other. What did I matter?"

"It wasn't like that at all. Please try to understand. Your mother loved you, but she also had a husband whom she dearly loved. Unfortunately, Nicholas Phillippi was not part of your grandfather's plan. He wanted her to marry someone prominent, from a good family, well educated, someone who could provide for her and maintain her in a standard of living to which she was accustomed. Not someone like your father, a wig maker. He never forgave your mother for marrying against his wishes." Her eyes brimmed with tears, but none spilled over.

"You know, Aunt Ro, the few times you took me there, I remember he looked at me with such repugnance. I didn't know that word as a child, but when I grew up, it was the word that best described it. Repugnance! Do you remember?"

"Yes, yes, Emmett, I remember. When he looked at you, he saw your father."

"I was always scared of him. I'd get sick to my stomach before going. And then I sat there silent, unmoving, quaking inside. I felt like a tiny bug, afraid he would reach out with those long gnarled fingers and squash me. Yet I was a good boy, a polite boy."

"You were, Emmett, and I was always trying to patch things up. There's no rhyme or reason for that kind of hatred. Innocent people are trampled by that kind of treachery. Your mother was his favorite, not I. And when she defied him, he hated the intruder with a vengeance. It destroyed him."

"It destroyed me," he quickly added.

"No, Emmett." She patted his arm. "*You* are a survivor."

He rose with a question on his lips. "Why didn't you tell me this before?"

"Would it have mattered? Would you have structured your life any differently? I think not. You had a sense of security, albeit a false one."

He bent over, kissing her cheek, the loose skin like accordion pleats, crumpled and pale. He picked up his coat. "I'll lock up. I'll try to visit tomorrow."

He left the brownstone with shattered confidence. He felt worthless. His own family despised him. If he died tomorrow, nobody would miss him. *Stop feeling sorry for yourself,* he reprimanded himself. *Think! Think of something. Think of some plan.*

Immediately, he began to think of some way to keep Aunt Ro alive forever.

#

When Rocco called Emmett, they decided to meet at Aunt Rose's brownstone. They would have complete privacy there. Aunt Rose was upstairs, and Emmett dismissed Winsome for the day, telling her he was holding a secret strategy meeting. Winny reluctantly gathered up her belongings and left, grumbling under her breath.

"Don't complain," he told her. "You're still getting paid." He could still be generous with Aunt Ro's money.

But she didn't go home. She rang Millicent's bell instead, telling her, "That man practically threw me out... and Ms. Rose—she's getting weaker and weaker."

"Why did he throw you out?"

"Someone's coming for a 'stragedy' meetin." Millicent didn't correct her.

"Do you think he's giving Rose something to knock the pins from under her?"

"Could be. I wouldn't put anything past that man when it comes to money. He's on his last fling, and he gonna make it or die."

"Let's watch at the window."

They moved to the window and saw Rocco arrive. "He looks like mob people," Winsome said with a laugh.

#

Emmett showed him in and escorted him to the living room, gesturing for him to take a seat. He sat down across from him and opened the conversation. "My man barely remembers this woman, and he remembers things much differently than she does."

"Fine," Rocco said calmly. "Than what am I doing here?"

"You're here because any hint of scandal, even imagined scandal, can be detrimental to this campaign. Because of the time element involved, we can't take a chance. How much does she want, and how long do we have to get it?"

Rocco sat across from him, his muscular legs spread apart, planted solidly like tree trunks. He leaned toward Emmett and examined his face. "Do you think this is about money?"

"Isn't it?"

"No. She wants your man to withdraw. That's her deal. She doesn't care what you tell the public. Say anything—illness, marital woes, lack of funds, whatever. She just wants him out."

Emmett's mouth felt dry and brackish. "Is this a Wilkens scheme? Did he dig her up? I know about you, Prevetti. I researched you. You're a sleaze."

"Takes one to know one," the unflappable detective answered. "What's it gonna be? Does he step aside, or does she go to the media?"

"I'll have to let you know."

They didn't waste one second or one word. They meant business.

"You have twenty-four hours." Rocco rose and walked to the door, closing it behind him.

Emmett remained seated. This was a replay of things before. Scandal was anathema to a political career unless you were rich and liberal. Those men usually overcame it. But a conservative? Never! The people expected more from a man with a polished image. It would have been better to pay her and take the chance.

His head hung as he desperately tried to jumpstart his analytical mind. The Wilkens camp and Prevetti knew of Laura Bartell, so he couldn't even think of getting rid of her, although it crossed his mind. This was an unsalvageable situation, and ultimately, it was Waverly's fault. His image was built on a lie. He had lied about his past and about being sterile.

Emmett felt betrayed by everyone: Waverly, his family. The only one who cared about him was Martine, and she had betrayed him by dying.

Prevetti was right. They were finished! All they could do now was back away without too much fuss and salvage their credibility. Maybe Emmett could latch onto someone else who could sweep the public with his charm, but he thought about all the average-looking, dull men trying to make it in politics, and he knew there would never be another Waverly Hampton.

#

When Lily started to replay the phone messages and heard Laura's, the name rang a bell. It was the same name mentioned by the pushy old guy in Queens.

She and Waverly argued over it. They had been doing that a lot lately. The plain wife was alarmed at all the attention that her handsome husband was getting from women. Political groupies were fawning over him, brazenly giving him their numbers, knowing the wife was just a few feet away. She hated all of it. Hostility lurked beneath the surface. Her imagination was running away; she was seeing him in all kinds of perverted sex acts with those bimbos. She wanted to try them herself, try different things with him, introduce him to more than what they had; but she was afraid he'd lose respect for her. He was always so fine.

So they continued with their unadventuresome sex life whenever they had time. Husband and wife were afraid to go one step further, but she played them in her mind. She played all the perverted sex scenes just like a movie, showing her husband with all those other women; and gradually, she talked herself into a jealous rage, arguing and accusing him of being unfaithful—and she wasn't wrong.

"You don't touch me anymore. You don't come near me anymore. Is Laura in town? You know, your college sweetheart? Is she in town doing all kinds of perversions to you?"

He refused to answer her. The blackmail was already taking its toll, and he became sullen. But Lily imagined something else—that he was hiding things from her.

It was one of these mornings, after an argument of accusations and denials, that she packed a bag and flew to Rochester to visit her parents, canceling all engagements. *I'll show him just how important I am to his primaries. I've had enough of Emmett, the campaign, the politics, the groupies, and him!*

She needed to be with her family and the magnificent house they lived in, the house that had impressed Way Hampton years ago. She wanted the life they'd had before the media circus, so she took off, and Way didn't stop her. He was glad. With all his problems, he was worn out reassuring her of his faithfulness, worried that she would find out about his tryst with the blonde volunteer and the blackmail. Life had a way of equalizing people. When you thought you had it all, you got kicked in the teeth.

But thank god, Emmett was there, calmly fielding questions about other issues. He trusted him to do damage control for the "Laura thing."

Then his private line rang. It was Emmett.

"Good timing." He forced cheerfulness. "I'm just about to step into the shower. Lily went upstate to her folks, thank god. She needs to get away. She's been driving me mad."

"Good. It's better if she's not around." But Emmett didn't call to chitchat; he called to tell him about Laura's demands.

"Did you speak with Laura?" Way asked.

"No, with her intermediary, a private eye."

"How much does she want?"

"Nothing. She doesn't want money."

"Great! Does she want an apology? Does she want to see me again? I charmed her once. I can do it again," he spoke flippantly, his outlook suddenly brighter.

"No, she wants none of that." He paused. "She wants you to withdraw."

There was a short silence before Waverly responded, "Is she nuts? I'm the favorite in this race. Wilkens doesn't have a chance. He's coming across as a nasty old man, and I'm getting the undecided vote. Do you hear me? I've got it! I'll be the conservative and Republican candidate. Is the woman nuts?"

"Calm down, Waverly. There's no argument. I agree with you. But if you don't withdraw, she will expose you, quote, 'as the hypocrite you are!' You lied to me, Way. You broke a trust. I put everything I had into you: time, money, energy, and expertise. I wouldn't have done it if I had known about your past. You lied to me and hurt me deeply. You said you were sterile. Was that supposed to be a smoke screen in case you were ever accused?"

"No, I wanted to spare Lily embarrassment. That's all."

The little man was calm, knowing there was nothing to do but withdraw. "Very noble. Now do another noble thing and withdraw. I'll try to pick up with someone else, but you can be rest assured they'll take a lie detector test."

"I'm sorry, Emmett. I really didn't remember her. I blocked it out."

"Too bad because it's come back to haunt you *and* me. There's no recourse. Wilkens knows about it."

"My god," Way murmured. "Did he find her?"

"Possibly, but he won't say a word if you withdraw quickly and quietly. Perhaps we can salvage our self-respect and do the talk circuit or write a book. You're easy to market. You don't look like a hypocrite." He didn't try to hide the sarcasm as he spoke those words. "As long as you withdraw from the race, nothing will come out. That was the deal."

"Emmett, you do stupid things when you're young and ambitious."

"You also do stupid things when you're old and ambitious," the older man replied.

"I won't withdraw. I'll ride it out. I *can't* withdraw. It'll be my word against hers. I didn't come this far to be scared off by threats of blackmail."

"Suit yourself. But she has witnesses to corroborate her story. After all, she ended up in a hospital—alone. Then you're finished. If you withdraw, we can still continue, perhaps get a book out of your rise from obscurity, get you on the lecture circuit, wait a few years, and try again. Maybe this woman will disappear. People do disappear in time."

Waverly's eyes narrowed. "What do you mean by that?"

"She might leave the country, have an accident."

"With anybody's help, Emmett?"

Emmett was silent.

"You didn't have anything to do with that baby, did you? If you did, it's a classic case of the pot calling the kettle. Did you?"

"Of course not," Emmett replied, "and I'm offended that you would ask that."

"I'm sorry." After a long pause, he sighed. "Okay, suppose we do it your way, how do I withdraw?"

"Ill health, stress, marital problems. That would go over great with the ladies."

He thought for a minute. "I'm riding the crest. I'm on top. Why would I suddenly leave? It doesn't make sense. It's my word against hers. No, Emmett, I won't withdraw! Let's meet and talk this over because I won't withdraw."

There was a cold silence. Waverly heard him sigh, then ask, "You're certain about this?"

"Yes."

"Then get yourself another campaign manager." His voice was resigned, emotionless. "I've run out of ideas, and Clark Wilkens will cream you."

Emmett hung up, wondering why the younger man just didn't walk away with his credibility and start anew when things died down. If he continued, he would make Emmett a laughing stock in political circles. Emmett knew now that he'd been naive to take a politician's word on face value, not hiring an investigator to check him out. But he had no money for that.

Damn Aunt Rose. She put me in this position on the pretext that she was doing it for my own good, so I'll have something in my old age. I am old and I still have nothing! No income, no power, no dream.

He began to cry as he thought about his bleak future. Depending on her generosity, moving in with her, taking over the chores. Keeping her away from people, making certain nobody would ever influence her again. He had to be certain that she lived. He would devote his life to her in exchange for his security.

He bent over, holding his head. His stomach felt queasy, his mouth sour. Tears stung his eyes as he sobbed into his hands. He'd wanted to do this for Martine. Finally, he wanted her to be proud of him, and he couldn't even do that. He missed her, that gentle, lovely creature who had loved this plain, homely man.

I was good when you were with me, Martine! Why didn't I die instead of you? Why didn't it work that way? You gave so much, and I could never get it right for you. I could never make you proud of me the way I was so proud of you. Proud to walk with you, proud to be seen with you. You took care of me in life and in death. Everything worthwhile eluded me but you. You were the one good thing that ever happened to me, and then Waverly came along, but he messed up everything. What an utterly stupid man he turned out to be. He didn't deserve my friendship. He didn't deserve my help. He didn't deserve me.

He went to the bedroom and opened Martine's closet. Tears still rolling down his face. There in neat array were all her clothes, everything as she had left it: neatly arranged lines of shoes, leather bags perched on shelves, belts hanging like a technicolor waterfall. Hats and wigs were stored in rose-covered hat boxes, with drawstring handles.

He lifted the lid of one of the boxes, and a length of hair swirled and pinned like a Danish pastry lay on the bottom. He removed the sparkling pin and lifted one end, letting it fall to its full length as he wrapped it around his wrists, salt-and-pepper handcuffs linking him to the woman he adored. He touched the fragile silk of her size 6 dress, the rough skin on his fingers snagging the fabric. He lifted it to his cheek, rubbing his face over it, his stubble catching on. He breathed in deeply, smelling her scent.

He removed the satin hanger and laid the dress out on the bed, lying down beside it, touching and feeling it, rubbing his face over it, becoming aroused. His eyes glazed as he remembered her. He unzipped his fly, released his throbbing penis, and moved it over the sensuous fabric, writhing in ecstasy as he made love to her dress.

Chapter 22

Waverly sat there for at least twenty minutes, his mind in turmoil, his head hanging slack. He couldn't think! Emmett was always right. With his analytical mind, he was always right. Could he be right again? Was it over? After weeks of grueling work and pressure, this woman threatened everything. They had worked so hard: he, Emmett, the volunteers.

Lily would be easy. He could tell her their marriage was more important than the campaign, and she would happily fall for that.

But ambition was a bright flame, and although his was flickering, it wasn't out. He became morbid, thinking about the adulation about all he would have to give up. Why didn't Emmett take care of her? She'd never been very important to him. Their affair and engagement was what young people did. They just fell into that trap. *I was clever enough to break free.* And now this unimportant woman was changing the course of his life.

I can't think straight anymore. Perhaps I'll feel better after a shower. Perhaps a hot forceful shower massage would help him think. He rose and stripped his lean and muscular body. He stepped into the bathtub, adjusting the massage showerhead and turning on the water full blast.

He wasn't thinking. A strong surge of scalding water hit his face and neck, shocking his left carotid artery like a karate chop. He stumbled forward but lost his balance and crumbled in a heap, hitting his forehead on the back ledge of the tub.

His forehead rested on the ledge with his face down, blood trailing down the porcelain, collecting in a little pool at the bottom of the tub. There wasn't a lot of room for such a big man; his body filled up the tub. He still clasped the washcloth in his right hand while the scalding, pulsating water continued thrashing onto his legs, now an angry red. The bathroom was becoming a sauna. The scalding water flowed quickly down the open drain. He was stunned but still alive. Perhaps the cold porcelain would revive him.

#

A woman walked into the building with a group of ladies. There was a bridge game on three where the others got off, but she remained on the elevator and went to the fifth floor. She went directly to the Hampton apartment and put the key in the lock and entered, closing the door softly behind her. She looked around for him, then walked carefully toward the bedroom, and heard the shower in one of the bathrooms.

She was in luck. He was showering, so it would be easy. She quickly removed the poison, went to the refrigerator, and poured it into the juice bottle. Working with gloves, she put everything back into her bag.

As she was about to leave, she heard the porter vacuuming the common hall. *I'll wait until he's through. I can't risk being seen.* Hearing the sound of the shower, she knew she still had time.

Curiosity got the better of her, though, and she followed the sound to the bathroom door. Slowly opening it, she could barely see into that steam-filled room. Mist covered everything.

Waverly Hampton was lying there, his forehead smashed against the back ledge of the large square tub. How perfect! He must have slipped. He had a fatal accident. She felt his pulse. No, he was still alive. But she had trouble breathing in that moist, dank air.

We'll see what we can do about that.

She slowly took the washcloth tangled across his fingers and put it over the drain. She wedged his foot on top, making a stopper. The tub began to fill, the cloth unable to rise with the weight of his foot on it. She watched as the water reached his face. When it rose past his nose, she knew he was dead.

She closed the door and ran to the refrigerator, quickly throwing the tainted orange juice down the drain, running the water, rinsing the container, and tucking it in her bag. She had no more use for it. Her gloves were soaking wet, but she kept them on, leaving as quickly and quietly as she had entered before the neighbors complained of a flood on the fifth floor.

Walking out the main entrance, she dropped her bag to get the doorman's attention. He dashed over to pick it up. "Thank you." She smiled and walked into the sunshine, down the street and out of sight with her wet gloves.

Chapter 23

Detective Larry Finglas stepped out of the shower. He towel-dried his reddish-blond hair, which stuck up in spiky clumps resembling a porcupine. Then he wrapped the damp towel around his skinny waist, tucking in the ends. A tall scarecrow of a man, his six-feet-four-inch frame swayed gracefully as he walked onto the dusty parquet floor of his newly rented sublet.

He missed Sheila dreadfully, especially at times like this, when he felt cleansed and human, when all the dirt and evil he dealt with was washed away. He and Sheila often made love afterward while the kids played or watched TV. After having that incredible closeness with the woman he loved, he began to feel human, lost in his feelings. He looked in the foggy mirror and was glad he couldn't see his craggy face. He wasn't looking very good lately, losing weight, losing sleep, and looking every bit like a scarecrow. His transfer to a downtown precinct, the impending divorce, and the move from a big comfortable house in Bayside, Queens, to a crummy studio sublet on Third Avenue made for a lot of stress.

"Toity, toid, and toid," he would tell women in bars, flashing a wide gap-toothed smile with his big square teeth, purposely turning them off. That was okay with him since he wasn't ready for a new woman in his life. None were even close to Shelia in looks or class. God, how he missed her!

Padding around the floor, his footprints left a wet trail. He turned on the TV, and at the same moment, the telephone rang.

"Yeah... I knew I shouldn't have picked it up," he said, reaching for a pen and jotting things down on the pad next to the phone. "If it's an accident, why do you need me? C'mon, Ned. It's my day off." It wasn't his weekend with the kids, so he had nothing planned. "Big stuff, huh? Okay, man, you'll never let me forget it. What's the address? Okay, I'll be there," he spoke with resignation and hung up.

How convenient this crummy little apartment was. He would dress and be there in twenty minutes. It would have taken him hours if he still lived in Queens. "You have to look on the good side of things. Otherwise, you won't survive."

He wondered why his buddy had called him. It was a fatal accident, not a homicide. "The victim was well-known. I guess they have to be sure. Maybe some rival offed him 'cause he was cutting into his votes."

He laughed as he pulled on a pair of trousers and reached for his navy blazer, then scurried out on Third Avenue, and hailed a cab.

#

The block had been turned into Times Square at New Year's Eve. Cop cars, ambulances, medical examiner's wagon, TV trucks with the stations' logos, satellite dishes, and cellular phones. Journalists, foreign and home grown, were all over the place. People could not pass in the street. The area was littered with butts and containers. *What the hell?* thought Larry.

"We're waiting for the return of the widow Hampton," one reporter told him. "We want to see her reaction."

"We want to see Wilkens's reaction too," another reporter called out.

"Hey, guys," Larry said, "it was an accident."

"Sure it was," they answered with a wink.

You may be right. Larry thought as he entered the building. The building personnel felt important because of all the excitement. Finglas flashed his badge.

"Five-L is where all the action is," the doorman said.

"Thanks." He walked across the cold marble floor and over a fake Persian rug. He looked at the two leather sofas that made a square sitting area. Hunting scenes with dark-green matting were scattered about. He expected a better-looking lobby in such an upscale building. It looked like the decorator had aimed for Old World elegance and missed.

He greeted a few young policemen on the way to the elevator and pushed the button to five. He wondered who found the victim. He was alone, showering, and slipped. His wife was away. So who found him? How did they know?

He discovered the answer as soon as he stepped onto the carpeted hallway. The carpeting was soaked. As he neared 5L, he heard the sound of the water vac sucking up the minilake. He entered, flashed his badge, and asked for Ned Cannon, spotting him immediately. Cops, EMS, and building personnel were all over the place.

"Ned, you old bastard, you couldn't give me a day off?" he joked.

"Larry, me boy, thanks for comin'." He lowered his voice. "Something's not clickin'. Put my mind at ease, will ya? I'll buy you supper. I'm sorry about you and Sheila."

"She's findin' herself."

"Come on, I want you to see this. Waverly Hampton, the prolife candidate."

107

"Too bad he didn't protect his own life." They sloshed over the soaked carpeting and went into the bathroom, the bottoms of their trousers getting wet.

"I should have told you to wear boots."

"How long before anyone noticed the water?"

"About twenty-four hours. It took that long for the apartment to become a pool and spill into the hall, where the neighbors got worried. There were repeated messages on his answering machine from his wife and manager. What a stupid accident." He shook his head.

"Yeah. Eighty percent of all accidents happen at home, in the kitchen or bathroom."

"I'm not so sure about this one," Ned replied.

"Those are the stats."

"I don't mean that, Larry. I mean I'm not so sure this was an accident. That's why I asked you to come. You're a great homicide detective, and I wanna bounce some things off you." He waved off a couple of cops. "Outta here, boys, 'til we're finished!"

They were in the bathroom, looking at the waterlogged corpse with calm detachment.

"Larry, crimes involve secrets with people intent on covering them up. Maybe I'm nuts, but someone could have disguised what really happened to make it look like an accident. There were a lot of people not happy with his popularity. He was showering. Look."

They stooped over to examine the body, which looked like a lobster that had been plunged into boiling water. He lay crumpled, facing the far wall.

"There was a cut and bruise on the forehead. The ME said it wasn't deep enough to kill him. To stun him perhaps but not kill him. He'll check further, but it appears that Hampton drowned. His face was down in the tub, hanging by his forehead off the back ledge. Now this is what bothers me. Why drown if you're taking a shower? The drain was open, right? When you shower, the drain is open."

"And this drain was closed?" Finglas asked.

"No, it was open, but his washcloth covered it, with his foot wedged on top. He was too heavy for the buoyancy to lift it. Now this is what bothers me. How did the washcloth get under his foot?"

"When he slipped?" Larry leaned over and looked at the body. A glob of mush that had once been soap was stuck on the inside of the tub near Hampton's upper torso. If he fell while holding both soap and cloth, both would have been in that area, the cloth probably floating out of the tub when the water spilled over.

"How could the cloth get past the barrier of his knees, which blocked passage downward? You get my drift?" Ned asked. "How could the cloth just float down, take a nosedive over the drain, and end up with his foot wedged on top? It doesn't make sense."

"He might have slipped on the cloth, kicking it back."

"Possibly, but then it would be kicked up and away, on top of his foot. It's too pat too carefully done."

Larry thought for a minute, visualizing the scene. "You're right. Any tampering with the locks?"

"Who knows? The manager let us in. They were all in and out the minute neighbors complained."

"Who would have a motive?"

"Political rivals. He was the spoiler for Wilkens. Prochoicers, feminists, a wife, a girlfriend, a colleague, a nut—who knows? He was steamrollin' along, flattening everybody." Then, without much conviction, "Of course, it *could* be an accident." He reached over and brushed the dandruff that littered Larry's shoulders.

"I should have worn gray," Larry apologized. "It would've blended in."

"That's it, pal. It doesn't blend. The washcloth bothers me, and yet I have nothing to go on but a hunch, a feeling. You know how it is, Larry. A scent, a little finger beckoning, something subtle. But it's telling you something. It's tellin' ya something's not right. I'd like you to be there when I talk to the major players."

"Sure, Ned. You could be on target. Who's to know, with this pool? It washed away a lot of clues. If it's murder, it's a clever one. Come on. Let's do our job so we can get outta here and eat something."

The Rochester police were contacted immediately and went to Mrs. Hampton's family to inform her. She stood up very well, the reality not settling in. She and her parents left Rochester at once and would be in New York within hours.

Emmett hurried over, stunned at the scene, a huge void in his life. It was final—it was all over. He answered questions.

"I wondered why Waverly didn't return my calls. I knew Mrs. Hampton was visiting her parents, and I thought he might have gone along."

"Didn't he tell you of his movements?"

"Yes, but they were both under a lot of pressure, and the marriage was strained. I thought they just went somewhere on the spur of the moment."

He sat in the chair, visibly shaken, his head in his hands, surrounded by the slushy carpeting. He thought of all the time, money, and work he had devoted molding this man who was now being stuffed into a body bag. Opportunity and circumstances presented themselves, and he had been smart enough to take quick advantage of the press to engineer the campaign from its inception to the respected position it was in.

Now, he had nothing. *How could you mess things up when we were so close?* he thought. He was angry at the blackmail, angry at the accident. Everything was lost! Waverly was a fool, and that fool spoiled everything!

I thought I would make it this time, my love, but once again I was thwarted by fate, he muttered. Once again, success had eluded him. He would never have another ride like this. There would never be another Waverly Hampton.

Chapter 24

The detectives were in limbo. They couldn't treat the Hampton death as a murder since it was an apparent accident. But there was something so pat about it, and the hunches and doubts nagged at them.

If someone had a key, they had to be on very close terms with Waverly Hampton. His wife was away. Was he seeing another woman for a matinee? They questioned Emmett again.

"No, I don't have a key to his apartment."

"But you could easily get one?"

"Yes, I suppose so if I needed it, but I never needed one."

"Was the deceased using an escort service or seeing another woman or man? How about a cleaning lady? Did anyone have a vendetta against him, any prochoice people?"

"Not that I know of... but of course, some nut did kill doctors in Florida. It could be a reversed-revenge thing."

He would conceal the blackmail at all costs, not wanting to smear Waverly's name, not wanting to make a fool of himself. If there would be a next time, he would be more thorough, hire Prevetti to do a background check on the candidate. Prevetti was slimy, but he was good.

Emmett started to feel optimistic about his future; two days ago, everything had looked so bleak. But now he was fielding calls from the press, returning their calls, acting as family spokesman. It was like old times.

Clark Wilkens gave a terse message of sympathy. He was now the big fish. He kept his word about the blackmail, and the police delicately checked his whereabouts. Privately, Wilkens couldn't contain his glee. This was much easier than having to deal with the blackmail. He felt that somehow Waverly would have wrangled himself out of that tight spot. He and Emmett had been a formidable team. A few tears were all it would have taken, a few public apologies with a doting wife on one side and his minister on the other, giving testimony about a changed man who saw the error of his ways. Because of the traumatic experience and all the guilt he carried around for years, he would have said he now wanted to spare others from making the same mistake.

Somehow, Wilkens thought, *he would have wormed his way out of it. A timely accident was much better.* He would discontinue the services of Rocco Prevetti, but he'd give him a bonus and kept his number handy for future reference.

The police also discreetly checked out Lily Hampton. Rochester was only forty-five minutes from New York City by plane. They heard of their marital problems caused by Waverly's newfound celebrity, and they grilled the campaign workers, asking if any of the women saw the deceased socially. "No," came the reply. The blonde volunteer kept silent. They checked out the cleaning lady, building personnel, the visitors for that day. But they came up empty.

Lily handled everything with great equanimity. She had known that the rift would grow between them as her husband's success grew. She had no longer been important to him. It was just a matter of time before she would have been shut out completely. Marriage meant nothing to ambitious men.

Laura Bartell was vindicated. She didn't care how Waverly stayed out of the race as long as he stayed out. If it took a fatal accident to do it, so be it! It had taken many years, many memories, many tears, and many hours of self-pity to finally reach the pure hatred she felt for this man. Men were such swine, and he was the worst of the lot. She began to feel better.

Aunt Rose felt defeated. She had hoped Emmett would finally have success while she was alive. Now, he would rely solely on her, getting in her way. He was her only living relative; and though she knew him to be a scoundrel, she rooted for him, hoping he would make it. But once again, luck eluded him with this stupid accident. With her friends gone, she would now have to rely on Millicent and Emmett, who would be hanging around more than ever, dictating to her. When she felt better, she just might go on a round-the-world cruise to get away.

Millicent finally had her old friend back. She visited Rose for tea, did some shopping for her, brought in her morning paper. Everyone else had disappeared.

Millicent wasn't great company, but she was a tad better than Emmett, who was morose and moody. He hoped some politician would hire him, but no one called. Millicent told Rose how sorry she was that it all came crashing down, but she wasn't that sorry since she had her old friend back. Millicent would spend time caring for Rose, who was becoming more frail and homebound.

Rose was now dependent on her and Winsome. They were her true friends; and it came as a shock when Emmett suddenly dismissed Winsome over the telephone, telling her that Aunt Rose had had a small stroke and she wasn't needed anymore.

"I'm hiring a private nurse, so we'll have to cut costs. I'm very sorry about this. I'm moving in to take care of Aunt Rose and the house."

Winsome immediately called Millicent, "He' gonna take care of her all right, probably keep her drugged and take over the place."

But Millicent had seen no sign of illness, no doctor coming and going, no ambulance. "If she had a stroke, he'd surely have the doctor over. I'm going over to check, but in the meantime, Winsome, you can work here the two extra days. I've got money. Maybe we just might be able to find out what his real intentions are."

With that, she hung up and went straight out the door to Rose's brownstone. She rang persistently and waited until Emmett opened the door. "Emmett, I hear Rosie's ill. I called several times. Why don't you answer the phone?"

"If I don't answer, it means I'm busy with Aunt Rose. She's had a slight stoke and is on medication, but she'll be up and around soon."

"Can I see her?"

"Afraid not. She's very drowsy from the medication, and she doesn't want visitors. You know how stubborn she can be. I'll let you know when you can come by. By the way, I was sorry to let Winny go. With Waverly's accident, I'm out of a job for the time being. I'm looking after Aunt Rose, and I'll be moving in permanently."

"But you're not a nurse. She needs a professional."

"I've hired a private nurse. That's why I let Winny go. We can't afford both."

"But she was with Rosie for twenty years! You don't just discard people."

"I had no choice, Melisande." He used her favored name to please her. "We can't afford both."

"Has a doctor seen her?"

"Yes," he lied.

"And what did he say?"

"It'll take time, but she'll improve."

"Give her my best, please, and if there's anything I can do, please call. Rosie and I have been friends for over fifty years."

"I know. Thank you." With that, he closed the door, barring her from seeing Aunt Rose. She didn't leave immediately but remained there another minute, staring into emptiness, a troubled frown on her face. Emmett had become an enigma. It was as if he was trying to keep Rose incommunicado. But why? Tomorrow, when Winsome arrived, she would find a way to get in and get to the bottom of things.

"I bet he has the place cleaned out," Winsome said.

"I'm worried about her. We've got to get in there."

"I'm worried about booby traps."

"I wouldn't put it past him. She's at his mercy."

"Did you ever see a nurse?" Winsome asked.

"Yes, I did see a woman leave once. I assume it was the nurse."

The two women went into the garden and looked up at the side window, where they saw a little of Aunt Rose's curly gray hair peeking out. "She's up! She must be sitting in her rocker. She's up!" They were annoyed. "Why did he lie to us?"

"Because he wants to keep her away from us," Winsome replied. "I have a key that he don't know about. Ms. Rose gave me an emergency key."

"Winsome, you're wonderful." Millicent grabbed the plump woman and hugged her. She was beginning to enjoy the detective work. It was more fun than the soaps.

"He don't ask, so I don't tell. I've had it fifteen years." She rummaged through her bag. "I was gonna return it but not now!"

"Maybe you should give it to me. I'm here when he leaves and returns. I wonder if he has power of attorney. If she's being held incommunicado, we've got to help her. I'll call my friend Mauritz. He helped the police smash a drug ring. He'll know what to do. But in the meantime, Winsome, you watch at the front window and see if he leaves or if he did indeed hire a nurse. But watch that house! That's your job for today."

"That's it?" Winsome asked. "No cleanin'?"

"No. The house is clean. You just watch. That's your job."

A half hour later, Winsome called in a loud whisper, "Ms. Millicent, he just left. Emmett just left!"

They couldn't believe their luck. They opened the door a crack and peeked out, their faces hidden by the planters.

"There he goes, up the street."

"Do you have the key?"

"It just so happens." A proud Winsome whipped it out of her pocket.

"Let's go. He may be going for the paper, or he may be going for the day." She pushed Winsome out the door and scrambled up the concrete steps next door, with Millicent on the lookout. The sun had put in a cameo appearance, but now it was completely overcast. Millicent trembled and pulled her sweater more tightly around her as Winsome slid the key in the lock and turned it. It didn't budge. She jiggled it back and forth, removed it, and tried to insert it upside down; but it didn't work.

"Let me try." Millicent exchanged places with her, yanked the key out, and slid it in again; but nothing moved. She was afraid to exert too much pressure, afraid it might break. "Do you have the right key?"

"Yes, the same one for fifteen years."

"Did she ever have the locks changed?"

"She woulda tol' me." Winsome leaned over and peered closely at the heavy Yale lock, the shiny brass finish gleaming in the sun. "This looks kinda new."

"It is new," a voice spoke behind them. They turned quickly to see Emmett holding a newspaper under his arm, watching them. "What are you doing?"

Winsome's heart pounded. She was so frightened. But Millicent spoke calmly, "We rang the bell, Emmett, and no one answered. So we tried to get in, afraid something had happened."

"Nothing happened. I just went for a paper."

"Where's the nurse? Why didn't she answer?"

"She's off today. Now let me tell you what I think. I think you're just nosy." He put out his hand. "Give me that key." Winsome dropped it into his palm. "If you don't stop harassing us, I'll take legal action against both of you." With that, he put his key in the lock, entered his house, and slammed the door in their faces.

The disappointed women just stood there for a minute, conscious of his eyes watching them.

"Winny, that was the dumbest thing he could have said to us," Millicent whispered. "Come on." She took the woman by the hand and led her down the steps and into her house next door.

Winny grumbled that the rescue mission had failed.

"Not so, just a slight delay in plans," Millicent said. "He must have changed the lock on a Tuesday, when I go to bridge. He knows that. Otherwise, I would have seen it. But, Winny, we are not finished with him, not for a minute. We are gonna fix him good. When my father died, I promised myself I would never again be bullied by another man. As much as I loved my father, I didn't like him very much." She went to the desk, looked up a number, and dialed. "I'm going to call Mauritz. He knows some top detectives in this city, and he'll know what to do."

The phone rang several times before it was answered.

"Mauritz? Hello, this is Melisande." She went on to explain everything. "An abuse of power of attorney must be handled delicately because he threatened me with a lawsuit, which didn't sit too well with me. Someone has to check on that poor old woman. We think he's drugged her and is holding her prisoner in her own home while he plays lord of the manor."

"I'll have Detective Larry Finglas call you, Millicent," Mauritz promised.

"Melisande," she corrected.

"Sorry, dear Melisande. It takes getting used to. One day it'll take hold. I'll have Detective Finglas call, but be patient. He's a very busy man."

"Thank you, Mauritz. I knew I could count on you for help."

"My pleasure, Melisande." A wry smile came across his elegant old face, knowing how pleased she would be that he got it right this time.

"Thank you, Mauritz," she answered, pleasantly surprised. Perhaps in a year or two, everyone would be calling her Melisande. She hung up, and the women poured a cup of tea while they waited. Both were on a mild high.

Larry Finglas called within the hour, and Millicent grabbed the phone on the first ring.

#

At the dismal gray end of the day, two detectives pulled up at the brownstone in an unmarked car. Larry Finglas had gotten the call from his old acquaintance, Mauritz, asking him to call a Millicent Foster, who was afraid her elderly friend was imprisoned in her own house by a greedy nephew.

When Larry heard Emmett's name, he became interested. He had seen Emmett at the Hampton apartment the day Ned Cannon asked him over. He found Emmett to be an intense, humorless man, but Larry had to reserve judgment as the accident wasn't funny.

Still, there was a desperation about Emmett. Although he had an alibi, Larry got bad vibes from this man; so he patiently listened to Millicent and promised to look into the matter, especially after hearing that Emmett had threatened her with legal action.

This was not official police business, though, and there was no proof of foul play. It was just a concerned neighbor. It had to be handled cleverly and delicately. People did have a right to privacy. The detectives would have to tread carefully and bluff their way inside to make certain that Rose Parsons was not in any danger.

Millicent could not have picked a better man. Larry was a master. As they emerged, Finglas saw the curtain move in the house next door. *That must be the neighbor's house,* he thought and wondered if Emmett would recognize him from the Hampton accident.

The detectives climbed up the concrete steps and rang the bell. They waited. Larry leaned on the doorbell. There was no answer. He pounded on the door with his fist to give this visit importance. Finally, the peephole opened. "Yes?"

"Police, Mr. Phillippi. I'm holding up my badge. Can you see it?"

"Yes. What do you want?"

"We're here to see"—he looked at a paper—"Rose Parsons," he finished.

"That's my aunt. She's ill."

"Will you open the door, sir, so we can talk?"

"We can talk this way."

"No, we can't." The firmness in his voice told Emmett he meant business. "Open this door, sir. Otherwise, I will be forced to call for backup."

They heard the chain slowly sliding across, and the door opened. "Now, what is this about?"

"I'm Detective Finglas, and this is Detective Heilbron."

"We've met," Emmett said sternly, looking directly at Larry.

"You have a very concerned neighbor," Larry continued. "Nobody has seen your aunt for weeks, and they're concerned."

"She's very ill, Detective. She's had a stroke and can't have visitors. I'm taking care of her. Did that nosey Millicent call? Of course, she did. I needn't ask."

"She's asking for a lawsuit," he threatened, "and you are too."

It was the worst thing he could have said to the tough detective. When people cry foul and threaten lawsuits, they're usually covering up something. The intimidation didn't work. It only stoked the fires of curiosity, which are part of a good detective's makeup.

"Her doctor hasn't been informed of her illness. Why not?" Finglas asked.

"She called the doctor? What nerve, checking on us. We changed doctors. It was an emergency."

"What's his name?" He had pen in hand, ready to jot it down.

"I'll look it up. It's one of those foreign names, an Indian. I'll give you his name and number, and you can verify everything. Let's put an end to this imaginary nonsense once and for all. I am devoting myself to my aunt's care."

"May we come in?"

"There's no need for that!"

"Sir, if you refuse to let us come in, I'll be forced to use the warrant I'm carrying," he lied, "and you know what comes next."

"Then use it."

"I will." Finglas reached into his inner pocket without delay and fumbled for a few seconds, trying to find his phantom warrant.

Emmett looked smug. "Embarrassing, isn't it, when someone calls your bluff."

The detective leaned on the doorjamb with one hand, towering over Emmett. "Get one thing straight, Mr. Phillippi. You can cooperate or not. But Detective Heilbron will be back within the hour with a search warrant while I camp on your doorstep. We will get inside! Once there, we'll go through every inch of this place."

"Looking for what?" a startled Emmett asked.

"Nothing in particular, but it could be an awful nuisance."

They watched each other with unblinking eyes as a reluctant Emmett stepped aside. "I have nothing to hide. It's just annoying that we can't have our privacy."

Finglas tapped his partner in silent relief.

Millicent watched the whole scene from her doorway, peeking through the planters. She loved every second of it. Mauritz was right: Larry was tough.

The men walked into a clutter of art objects and DVDs strewn about. There were paperweights, snuff bottles, rare books, and paintings scattered in lots of four or five each, some on tables, some on the floor, or on the sofa. The police took it all in.

"Inventory," Emmett volunteered. "My uncle was a collector."

"For an auction?" Finglas asked.

"Eventually. It costs a lot of money to be sick."

Bullshit, Finglas thought. *The money's for you.*

"We'd like to speak to your aunt."

"Oh no, Detective. She's not up to it."

"She'd better be," the detective warned. "Otherwise, we'll be forced to call EMS to remove her."

"That Millicent," he said, shaking his head in disgust. "My aunt is not well. She is sleeping, and I'm not going to disturb her. Her rest is important."

"Mr. Phillippi, we're not leaving 'til we see your aunt. Now, you allowed us in, so why don't you just cooperate and let us have a peek? It'll put an end to all the innuendo."

"Which is?" he quickly asked.

"That you're keeping your aunt sedated for financial control."

"Nonsense, utter nonsense. Okay, Detective, if you insist. I'll disturb the poor lady. You'll have to excuse me while I wake up my aunt. I'll call down when she's ready."

Emmett climbed the stairs, leaving the two men standing there. The minute he was out of sight, they started poking around. "Comes with the territory," they joked and walked into the kitchen, where more clusters of artifacts, bronzes, jades, and ivories decorated the large kitchen table. A yellow notepad was nearby for cataloging everything, one quarter of the written pages turned under. Emmett had been a busy man.

"No wonder he doesn't have time to answer the door," Finglas observed. "He's getting ready for a sale at Sotheby's."

"Looks that way," his partner agreed. "Well, there's nothing illegal in cataloging your own valuables. Check the dining and living rooms." He picked up a DVD. "Never went out. Stayed home and watched all these old movies."

Then Finglas tried to open a locked door. He snapped the lock, and it opened, leading to the basement. He switched on the light, and the smell of mildew reached his nostrils as he descended to the cool, damp belly of the building. "Mushrooms would grow here," he muttered. The low-wattage bulb gave of an eerie glow, casting forms and shadows against the concrete walls. He poked around, looking inside the washer, which was empty and dry. Some grimy-looking clothes were still hanging over the clothesline. He touched them, but they were stiff as a board. *Needs fabric softener,* he thought. He'd learned all about that stuff since the divorce.

His head shot up as he heard footsteps, then recognized his partner's feet. "I'm getting jumpy." There was something eerily unpleasant about this place. "You could throw a great Halloween party down here," he joked.

"Forget Halloween." The younger man was getting anxious. "If he finds out we're bluffin', he'll have our asses."

"Let's not let him find out."

"I don't know why I let you talk me into this shit."

"'Cause your life's dull, and I promised you excitement."

"This is excitement? What's takin' so long?"

"She's gotta get prettied up. Or if he's drugged her, he's gotta revive her. After all, we weren't expected. That's the neighbor's feeling. He keeps the rich old aunt a vegetable while he takes over lock, stock, and barrel. From the looks of things, I think we interrupted a takeover. In time, the neglected old woman conveniently dies of natural causes. He's off the hook. He has power of attorney and inherits the whole shebang."

"Did you look in the freezer?"

"Not yet. Maybe we'll find a body." He laughed.

They quickly moved to the big white freezer and opened it, finding neatly stacked packages of frozen food. It seemed very innocent. They removed a few layers, but there was nothing suspicious.

Finglas motioned with his head, and they quietly climbed the stairs to the kitchen. They sat down at the table, occasionally picking up one of the objects d'art to examine it. "They don't make stuff like this anymore."

They waited. A half hour passed and still no word from Emmett.

"You think he killed himself?" Heilbron asked. "I don't hear nothing."

"Yeah, it's too quiet." Finglas rose and called up the staircase, "Mr. Phillippi? Is everything all right?"

"Yes," he called down. "She wants to be prettied up. She'll be ready in a few minutes."

They rolled their eyes and shrugged.

"Let's get on with it," Heilbron said, looking at his watch, his mouth tightly stretched.

"He probably is reviving her. We'll try to get a blood sample and call EMS. They'll be here in a couple of minutes."

"Lots a luck." The younger man laughed.

"Okay, in a couple of hours." Larry joined him. "When I speak to her, don't take your eyes off him. I don't want him intimidating her."

Suddenly Emmett called down, "Gentlemen, Aunt Ro is ready to receive you."

They rose and shuffled through the hall to the staircase, Finglas taking the lead. With each step, he felt an air of grim foreboding, and his heart pounded as they climbed in musty silence. When they reached the landing, his palms were sweaty, and his scalp crawled. Goose flesh like hobnails popped up as an icy feeling moved down his back. *What the hell is this?* he thought, ashamed to say anything to his partner.

Something didn't feel right, though, and Finglas had been a cop long enough to obey his instincts. He reached for his gun and ordered Heilbron to do the same, feeling guilty about dragging him into this. "Why didn't he come back down and escort us? Let's not get blown away by some nut."

But there was no ambush when they stepped into the dimly lit hallway. A light shone like a beacon from a room at the end of the dark hall, which was layered in shadows like a gloomy fabric hanging along the walls. "Jesus," Finglas finally admitted, "my scalp's creepin'. Do you think she's dead? You think he dressed up a corpse?"

"It's happened. You think he's nuts?"

"I dunno."

"In here, gentlemen," her sweet voice guided them.

They sighed in relief. "It's okay." They holstered their guns, keeping their hands near them as they cautiously walked into the old lady's room and relaxed when they saw her sitting in the rocking chair, wearing a burgundy robe and velour slippers, the gray hair neatly in place with makeup on her face. "Jesus," Finglas muttered, "these old ladies are all alike." The amber lamp cast a glow around her.

"Good evening, ma'am," Finglas said, eyes darting around the room, looking for Emmett.

"Good evening, gentlemen," she said in a weak voice, looking straight ahead. "It is indeed a lovely evening."

The air seemed thick as if there was something creepy going on, and Finglas could hardly breathe.

"Mrs. Parsons?" he spoke hesitantly.

"Yes."

"Where is your nephew?" he questioned, not trusting him.

She turned to him. "He's in the garden."

Finglas took a closer look at the old lady, and an icy tingle coursed down his spine. "Jesus Christ," he muttered. "It's just like the movie." Both men had suddenly entered the netherworld of evil fantasy.

"Where's your aunt, Mr. Phillippi?' he asked firmly.

"Here!" Emmett answered in Aunt Rose's gentle voice. He had taken great pains to recreate the old woman from her curly gray wig down to the velour slippers.

"Mr. Phillippi, *where* is your aunt?" His voice was firm.

"She's here," he insisted.

Finglas decided to play the game. "Then where is Emmett?"

"In the garden."

"With anybody?"

"With Kiwi. They're both in the garden."

"Jesus Christ, he murdered them," he said under his breath. "Is anyone in the freezer?"

"Noooo," Emmett answered, offended at the question. "They're in the garden."

"Who is Kiwi?"

"A former friend." The man stayed in character every second.

"Get a judge to issue a search warrant and call for backup," Finglas instructed his partner. "And tell them to bring shovels. We gotta find something before we can book him. But get the warrant."

Emmett's eyes widened for a second.

"Okay, but first I better look in the garden," Heilbron said. "They might just be havin' tea."

"Very funny, pal. Check it out, but I assure you, they're not havin' tea."

Within fifteen minutes five police cars responded, and within forty-five minutes, they had the warrant. When Finglas asked Emmett for the location, he said he didn't remember. Finglas immediately sized him up as being a clever game player.

Finglas directed them to start the search. He reasoned that they would be shallow graves, knowing that Emmett would have to work quickly and quietly not to alert the neighborhood.

The police worked without respite, hoping to beat nightfall, but a thorough search of the garden revealed nothing.

"Check the basement," Finglas ordered, sending men downstairs. "The freezer. Open the packages. Check for new paint jobs, loose concrete, or dirt. I don't have to tell you." He patted his partner's arm. "I promised you excitement, kid! You got it. I'm going next door to the neighbors. You guys stay with him."

As the detective turned to leave, Emmett complained indignantly, "I should have a matron assigned to me, not two men." Finglas laughed and really wondered about this guy. He would probably find the Hitchcock movie among the DVD collection. Life imitating art.

When he rang Millicent's bell, she opened the door immediately. He flashed his badge and introduced himself, "You should always ask, ma'am. Never open your door."

"I never do, Detective, but I've been watching, so I knew it was you. Come in." She stepped aside, allowing him to enter.

"So you're Mauritz's lady friend? Nice man, Mauritz."

"Yes, he's lovely."

"We met on a case, few years back, and stayed in touch."

"Have you found anything, Detective? I've been watching."

"The whole neighborhood's watching." He laughed. This was unusual for Murray Hill, with its landmark buildings and well-kept brownstones. It was a quiet neighborhood and the only precinct that had had no murders for a long time.

"We've found nothing. But I suspect that Rose Parsons is dead."

"Are you certain, Detective?" She found it curious. "Rose inherited a family trust that generated a nice income. It will cease on her death. The house will be sold, and everything will go to her father's favorite charities. It wouldn't benefit Emmett to kill her. He needed her alive for that income and to remain in the house."

"Did he know that?" Finglas cocked his head, intrigued with the circumstances. "I'm sure he did."

"Well, her nephew has taken her identity. He's dressed like her, wig and all."

"He what?" She was incredulous.

"He is pretending to be Rose Parsons."

"How ridiculous! Does he think he'll get away with it, pretending he's crazy?'"

"We'll see, ma'am. Has he ever displayed any bizarre behavior before? Could he really be insane?"

"Well, he's always been a little odd, always desperate for money." She pulled the ubiquitous sweater around her shoulders closely. "Brilliant but odd. Never successful, always full of schemes that didn't work. Rose rescued him financially many times. But a transvestite? Perhaps she died of natural causes, and he perpetuated the myth for his own security."

"It's possible, but we won't know that until we find a body. You noticed something strange going on?"

"Yes, that's why I called Mauritz. But it may answer a nagging question I had about the private nurse. I caught a glimpse of a woman about Emmett's height and build, coming and going a few times. Never saw her again. It might have been him."

"I'm sure it was. He couldn't give us the new doctor's name or the nurse's registry. He could have been an actor playing many roles. But he was cornered, thanks to you. I have to find out if it's a real psychosis or if he's bluffing."

"He's a very tricky man, Detective. Don't trust him."

"That I know, Ms. Foster, but so am I."

She smiled and had complete confidence in this man.

He followed her up the staircase to the well-appointed living room. What a feat of magic, this light modern, well-furnished house. He was surprised that this plain spinster had such modern taste. The light airiness of the house was a marked contrast to the bleakness of the house next door.

Finglas literally bounced across the light-gray carpeting. It was so lush and thick he could imagine its comfort while doing his exercises. The walls were a lighter shade of gray, a perfect backdrop for the contemporary gray, white, and black furniture that dotted the room. It was exquisitely modern. Finglas liked the track lights, which illuminated the large Erté prints. Elegant art deco ladies mysteriously peering out from the black-lacquered frames.

"You did a great job here," he complimented.

"When my father died, I gutted the whole place. Because I could do nothing while that man was alive. Every decision had to be his." She looked around at her handiwork. "I had fun doing this in spite of all the mess."

They walked into the cheerful kitchen, which had every modern appliance, from an ice water spigot to a pasta maker. Then they went out to the porch and looked into her small garden. Over the wall, they could hear the sounds of the police, still digging.

"You might be looking in the wrong garden, Detective," she said thoughtfully. "On several occasions, in the wee hours, I saw a man in my garden, kneeling, looking for something or doing something. I should have phoned the police, but I thought nothing of it. He went back into Rose's yard. I assumed it was one of her homeless friends wandering about, and they really didn't do anything wrong. Besides, I didn't want to get into trouble."

"What kind of trouble?"

She gave him a sideways look. "Mauritz said you're trustworthy."

"What kind of trouble?" he repeated.

"Mauritz said I can trust you."

"You can."

"Years ago, my father had a fifty-five-gallon drum buried in our garden. It was during the forties, when gasoline was rationed. It was filled with black market gasoline."

"That was dangerous, ma'am."

"I know." She pointed to a circle of bricks bordering a round cement stepping stone with a decorative raised relief pattern of a child and several bunnies. Grass grew around it and peeked through the bricks. It was a pretty garden design. "It's there! I've been terrified for years, afraid it would blow up in a lightning storm, afraid the authorities would come storming down on me. I've lived in fear."

"Does Phillippi know about it?"

"He might. His uncle was a pathologist, who chatted with Father. He may have told him. Will I get into trouble?"

"Melisande." He used her preferred name as Mauritz suggested. "I'm going to discover that drum all by myself. I'm going over to those bricks to poke around." He removed his Swiss army knife and pulled out the long blade as they walked to the circle.

The bricks seemed loose, the dirt not firmly packed between them. He stooped down and, using the knife, removed the bricks one by one, finally slipping the blade under the innocent circle of cement and lifting it. He felt a rush of adrenaline, realizing what he had found.

But the putrid smell of rotting flesh and fumes almost knocked him over. He quickly covered it and yelled to the men next door still milling around Emmett's garden to stop what they were doing and come over. In seconds, Millicent was opening her front door to more cops, who politely wiped their feet on the coconut coir mat. She loved it! She'd not had so much excitement since her father caught her in bed with her lover, and she was off the hook with the drum. Suddenly, life seemed brighter.

When the detectives reopened the drum, they all felt sorry for the pathologist who would have to work on the remains. They would need more than a mask to mask this stench. They would need Noxzema-dipped cotton rolls stuffed up their noses. That or a gas mask.

Finglas called off the search next door, leaving Emmett's garden looking like a rodent fest. Everything was uprooted: flowers, grass, shrubs, and trees. Anything green was thrown into one pile against the fence while the rest of the garden was a brown rectangle. Telephones rang, and police cars parked every which way littered the street. The traffic out of the midtown tunnel was snarled, with nosy strangers being caught up in this bizarre scene, rubbernecking as they passed. Neighbors stood in clusters, lining the street, asking questions of anyone exiting either house.

The medical examiner and forensics team arrived from just blocks away wearing navy-blue windbreakers with Office of Chief Medical Examiner splashed across the backs. The media started to arrive in vans, with their respective station's logo painted boldly on the sides. The street filled up with satellite dishes, cellular phones, and reporters trying to get a scoop. They were asking for Emmett, begging for an interview. They knew him from the campaign.

"Who's his lawyer? Who's his lawyer?" they called out. The once-peaceful street looked like the Feast of San Gennaro, a New York street fair.

"Nobody knows yet," they were told.

Millicent supplied coffee and snacks for the men, finally putting her modern kitchen to use. She wished Winsome was here to help. But it was late, and she knew Winny would be upset at the news. She would wait until morning.

A crane was ordered to lift out the drum. They wanted everything intact, so they waited for equipment, drinking gallons of coffee while Finglas sent two cops back to Emmett's to find the female clothes he'd used in the murders. They would need more evidence. Finglas wanted a list of every item and the sizes of any female clothes hanging there.

Finally, at 2:00 a.m., the crane arrived, coming in through the back. The operator, a pro, guided it close enough to the fence until the drum was finally lifted out, sealed, and taken to the lab, along with everyone's sympathy for the forensics team. They would have to examine the remains in detail to determine the cause of death.

Millicent hoped Rose had died of natural causes, and she was upset that her garden had been used as the burial ground. She was grateful to Finglas, though, for not getting her in trouble about the drum.

124

The drum held the remains of two females: Rose and Kiwi Quieter. There would be a positive ID after the forensic dentists compared Rose's dental charts. Kiwi probably had none. And there would be an autopsy to determine the causes of death.

They found something else, which Finglas never discussed: the remains of a mummified fetus, wrapped in oilcloth. It had to have been a long time ago—something she must have blocked out. He said nothing to her. *Let them think it was Kiwi's.*

Finglas woke up Ned Cannon and told him about Emmett in drag. The older detective found that very interesting and reconstructed the Hampton accident, remembering what the doorman at Waverly Hampton's apartment building had said.

"Several elderly women entered the building for their weekly bridge game, along with several tenants. But one woman left shortly afterward. The doorman remembered her because she'd dropped her purse, and he had picked it up. He knew she wasn't a tenant." Cannon paused. "I didn't think anything of it then, but I do now. I think he deliberately dropped the purse so we would look for a female."

"What about the baby's murder? Larry Finglas reminded him. "I wasn't on that case, but it was an elderly nurse that nobody could identify. Lots of old ladies running around murdering people! Ned, it's clicking into place. Good thing you called me on the Hampton accident 'cause it's turning out to be murder. Millicent Foster piqued my interest when she mentioned Philippi's name. Otherwise, I might not have pursued it so diligently. Hey, come on over, Ned. It was your nose that smelled a rat."

Shortly thereafter, Ned Cannon arrived. He was sleepy-eyed and pushed his way past cops and media until he found them.

"Do you remember me?" he asked as he approached Emmett. "I questioned you in Waverly Hampton's apartment."

"Oh no, that wasn't me," Emmett replied. "It was my nephew."

Larry rolled his eyes and shrugged at Ned. They set a tape recorder on the night table near the rocking chair, and Larry pushed the button to record.

"This is Detective Larry F. Finglas, and I'm interviewing Emmett Phillippi."

"My name is Rose Parsons," Emmett interrupted in his female voice "I'll start again. This is Detective Larry F. Finglas and I'm interviewing Emmett Phillippi impersonating his aunt Rose Parsons." Emmett was about to interrupt, but Larry pointed his finger at him, and he remained silent. The men stood on either side of him as Finglas read him his rights from the little card. "Were you the nurse who murdered the baby?"

"Yes, I did it for Emmett."

The detectives looked at each other, knowing that their work was cut out for them.

"Did you murder Waverly Hampton?"

"Yes. He lied to Emmett and said he was above reproach, said nobody could dig up anything on him. But the girl was going to blackmail him! Expose him!"

"What girl?"

"Laura... Laura Bartell, that tramp."

"Why?"

"For the abortion."

The cops exchanged looks as if they had found a land mine. Emmett continued in Aunt Rose's voice, leaning forward. The female attire and manner suited him.

"He made her have an abortion. She almost died. Then he left her. My, how she hated him." He shook his head in empathy, the silver waves catching the light.

"Was she going to blackmail him?"

"Yes, but not for cash. She just wanted him out of the race."

"This gets curiouser and curiouser." Finglas shook his head. "Did Clark Wilkens know any of this?"

"I'm not going to jeopardize that relationship by talking to the press about Clark Wilkens," Emmett replied in a huffy Aunt Rose voice.

"I'm a cop, not the press," Finglas said.

"Well, Wilkens just might hire Emmett for his next campaign. He was very impressed with him, you know. I certainly don't want to spoil that. There was nothing wrong with Emmett. It was Waverly Hampton who spoiled everything. He spoiled Emmett's big chance. Here was this brilliant man, my nephew, and that Waverly would have made him a laughing stock." Emmett was pathetically serious. "And the worst of it was that he wouldn't give up the race. Even if exposed, he thought he could beat it. At least the secret died with him, and Emmett saved face."

"Well, the secret's out now."

"Yes, and people will want to know everything."

"Did Emmett hit him?"

"Oh no, he fell. Emmett just covered the drain. I want you to know none of Emmett's murders were violent. Kiwi, Harry, and the two others—they went real quick, with the antifreeze in the wine."

Bingo, Finglas thought. *He made a slip.* Five minutes ago, Aunt Rose was claiming the murders, and now it was Emmett. Finglas looked at Cannon to see if he caught it. Larry wondered if this was all an act.

"What about your aunt Rose?"

"I'm Aunt Rose. He would never harm me. I will die one day of natural causes."

"How did you—" He rephrased, "How did Emmett kill the others?"

"With the antifreeze. He saw it on a TV show. Some brands taste sweet. That's why so many pets and children poison themselves. Perhaps we should have given the boy his mother's share of the inheritance," Emmett spoke wistfully, and they had it all on tape.

"What about the clothes you both wore?"

"All carefully burned in the basement." Emmett leaned forward, his voice conspiratorial. "The smoke alarm went off once, causing a terrible racket. We thought surely that nosy Millicent would call the fire department. He lost the blue sweater, though. In the hospital, someone must have picked it up. But Millicent gave him the idea, with that blue sweater always wrapped around her. He almost expected *her* to get arrested. Now wouldn't that have been fun?"

"We found other female attire and some wigs."

"They are mine."

"What size do you wear?"

"Sixteen."

"Are you certain they're yours?"

"Yes."

"Could they possibly have belonged to Emmett's late wife?"

"Some, but most are mine."

"But you're a sixteen, and they are all size 6."

"I use to be a 6. I saved them."

Finglas sighed with disgust. "Take this guy uptown and book him." Emmett was beginning to wear on him. Was it all an act, a way out if cornered? A clever man having an escape route planned in case they closed in? Not guilty by reason of insanity, but what better reason than insanity to get away with murder? *I'm going to find out if he had a history of being a cross dresser.* Were the female clothes his, or was he just hanging onto his wife's old clothes? He couldn't possibly wear a size 6.

But he had to be sure! Like Ned Cannon with Waverly's accident, he had a nagging doubt that Emmett was truly insane. He felt he was too clever for that. He thought Emmett would try an insanity plea to beat the rap or to gain notoriety. He had to know that the media was all over the street. People did crazy things for media coverage, hoping to get a book or a movie deal.

"Do you have a lawyer?"

"Oh yes, a brilliant one—Emmett!" Emmett answered.

Was he matching wits with the seasoned detective? Finglas thought of the campaign and how Emmett had operated with a flare that always found a diabolical way to accomplish a goal. This political mastermind took an unknown and made him a celebrity, harnessing the media. He wondered if Emmett would do it again, a celebrity in the making.

Finglas could imagine the scenario. A sympathetic judge would grant a release, and he would live off the spoils of his murders.

"Complete rehabilitation. He is no longer a danger to society," the judge would declare.

"Are you certain, Your Honor?"

"Absolutely! Mr. Phillippi answered every question correctly. He knew all the presidents, knew what day it was, even knew who *he* was. We must release him in time to get his book published." Case dismissed, he banged the gavel as Phillippi walked.

Finglas smirked at the thought. After the book, they would make a TV movie, telling the inside story of the deception. Another human experience sold for entertainment. Then onto the sleazy talk shows, finding his own celebrity at last. The law permitted this unreal world where careers were made or broken by the skill with which they could sway a judge or jury.

No, you creep, you're badly mistaken. I'm gonna make sure your plan never works. I'll match wits, lobby for the prosecution, get the best-damned psychiatrists to blow holes in your charade. I'll make it my mission to put you away forever in a prison for the criminally insane. I'll stop every goddamned plan! You have the media smarts, but I have the street-smarts.

Shored up by his enthusiasm to get Emmett, Finglas seemed refreshed, not tired at all after this long trying night. He fired instructions to his men. "Make sure they hold the crowd back. We have to protect this lady! Okay, ma'am, let's go," he spoke with phony politeness and rolled his eyes as he cuffed Emmett and led him down the stairs, through the dim hallway stripped of valuable paintings, past empty squares of lighter paint where they had once hung.

Heilbron walked ahead and opened the door to the blinding flash of cameras. He saw spots before him and blinked rapidly to clear his vision. The cameras clicked like noisy little insects. Hordes of people lunged forward, reporters and onlookers. It was a detective's nightmare, and the police were doing their best to keep an open path to the car.

Finglas and Emmett descended the concrete steps into the street, where the reporters pushed past the neighborhood people, who gasped, nudging one another, all eyes on this human anomaly. They shoved microphones in their faces. "We want an interview, Emmett, an exclusive," they yelled.

A smile played on his lips.

"Why did you do it, Emmett? What made you do it?"

"Did you really kill Waverly Hampton?"

"Detective, did you carry a search warrant? Did he give you any resistance?"

Emmett carried himself like a dowager queen. A faint smile crossed his horsey face as he slightly nodded to his subjects.

You must be in your glory, you crazy bastard, Finglas whispered between clenched teeth, his lips barely moving.

Emmett, still wearing Aunt Rose's clothes, minced along in her velour slippers, head held high. He stopped only to glare at Millicent, who glared right back and mouthed the word *murderer.*

Finglas didn't need a confrontation now, so he tugged him along and treated him as he would have treated an elderly woman: with gentle patience. He helped him into the backseat of the car, placing his hand on top of Emmett's wig, the standard police procedure. The police held back the curious crowd, which surged forward for a better look.

Emmett wiggled around, trying to get comfortable, his velour robe catching on the plush seat. Finally, he was comfortably seated. Finglas leaned his scrawny frame into the door and ran the back of his hand up Emmett's cheek, declaring war. "Phillippi, you need a shave!"

Emmett looked up, batted his eyelashes, lifted the corners of his mouth, stared out the window, and smiled for the cameras.

He wasn't through—yet! He had harnessed the power of the media for Waverly, and he could do it again for himself. Look at them all around him, firing questions, begging for interviews. *I'm an instant celebrity,* he thought. *Hardback, paperback, movies, tabloids, TV interviews, and an overturned Son of Sam law. Perfect! It will all be ours, Martine. You will finally be proud of me because this time I made it!*

And as the police car inched slowly past the throng of onlookers, he began plotting a plan to get himself out of this mess so that he could enjoy the fruits of what he felt was his enormous success!

FIN

Printed in the United States
By Bookmasters